THE RANCHER TAKES HIS BEST FRIEND'S SISTER

THE RANGERS OF PURPLE HEART RANCH BOOK 2

SHANAE JOHNSON

Edited by Alyssa Breck

Manufactured in the United States of America
First Edition March 2020

 *our years ago...*

"I keep telling you guys that girls are nothing but trouble."

Grizz agreed with the words of his best friend. Not because Keaton was his best friend. It was because Grizz knew the girls eyeing him at this party were mostly underage. True, about two-thirds of them were seventeen with just a few days or months until they were of legal age. The truth of the matter was that their minds were still wrapped around high school issues, final exams, who was dating whom, and what they would be doing for the rest of their lives.

But that's what he got for hanging around at a high school graduation party at twenty-one. Grizz had aced all his exams in high school, he'd had to. It was the only way he would have a future. He already knew what he was doing for the rest of his life. Dating was not a part of the plan.

"I don't plan to get married for at least five years after I'm out of the service." Keaton ran his hand over his buzz cut, courtesy of the United States Army.

Grizz scrubbed his fingers through his short-cropped hair and then across his chin. There was already stubble there even though they'd only been on leave for a few days.

Grizz didn't plan on ever getting married. His mother had always said he had too much of his dad in him. Malcolm Hayes had never been able to stay put for more than a couple of weeks, a month if they were lucky.

Amanda Hayes divorced his father and then proceeded to work all hours of the day and night to repay the debt the man had left them in. His mom's workaholic tendencies also left Grizz mostly unsupervised as a kid. Grizz hadn't gone in search of trouble. But as the child of a single mom, he was an easy target for trouble to find.

"But she's the one." That moan came from the third person in their group. Mac Kenzie also scrubbed his hands through his blond spiked hair. The tendrils were curly when they were long, but after they'd been kissed by a razor, they stuck straight up. The man, who had enough muscle to spare for a weight set, crossed his arms over his broad chest and pouted.

Grizz wasn't the only one trouble had found. But unlike him, Mac's trouble didn't follow him around on the streets. Mac followed his own special brand of torture around begging for her to kick him in the heart again and again.

"It was love at first sight with her," Mac continued. "I knew it the moment I saw her that I would spend the rest of my life with her."

"So, where is she tonight?" asked Keaton. Keaton wasn't being mean. At least not on purpose. He had always preferred things to be concrete. He liked to plan.

Mac kicked at a rock. "She had to work late."

"Seems to me she's more into her job than she is into you," said Keaton.

"For now," said Mac. There was a knowing gleam

in Mac's eyes that Grizz only ever saw when the big man was planning something crazy in the field, something that usually blew up all over their faces.

"You asked her to marry you again," said Grizz. "Didn't you?"

Mac didn't answer.

"I take it you got the same answer as the first five times?" said Keaton.

"Wrong," said Mac.

Both Keaton and Grizz turned to their friend with interest in this change of events. Mac's glee was short-lived.

"I've only asked her four times," he confessed.

"Well," said Grizz. "I'm sure the fifth time will be the charm then."

Mac brightened. "You think?"

Keaton and Grizz shared another look. Mac was the jokester of their group. Except when it came to this particular topic. He could never see the irony. He couldn't see anything when it came to this girl. But it looked like he was going to catch on this time.

Mac's features morphed from clear rapture to cloudy confusion and then stormy indignation.

"Just wait until it happens to you," said Mac. "With how tightly you're wound, Keaton, love will definitely knock you on that big head of yours. And I'll bet it'll happen within five years."

Keaton scoffed. He wasn't so rigid as to believe his plans would work perfectly. But, he planned for so many contingencies that things rarely strayed far from his expectations. Anthony Keaton was rarely surprised or caught off guard.

"And you, Grizz," Mac continued, "with how thick you two thieves are? You're going down soon after him."

Grizz didn't bother to answer. He may not have a lot of contingencies in his life plan, but this one thing he knew for sure.

Unlike his father, Grizz had no debts. He owed no one. He handled all of his responsibilities.

But where he resembled his old man was in his inability to hold still. Which wreaked havoc on any potential relationship. Which was why he had never been with a girl for longer than a month. They simply couldn't hold his attention.

Grizz could hardly hold still, which was why the army suited him. After the drilling of Basic Training, which kept him on his toes, he was never bored working twelve-hour days and being on call for the other twelve. He would often wake up in a new and exotic locale. But he craved even more, which was why he and his friends would all be taking the Army Ranger Exam soon.

With his restless spirit, Grizz knew he would never make a good family man. Which was fine, because he'd long ago decided he wouldn't become a father or a husband. He'd be free to travel the world with nothing tethering him to a single spot.

His gaze lifted as though tugged by an invisible force. She was a force to be reckoned with, all right. Wherever Patricia Keaton moved in a room, Grizz could always pinpoint her exact location.

She was dressed in a simple sundress and sandals, but she could've been a model walking right out of a fifties family drama, like *Leave it to Beaver* or *The Donna Reid Show*. Those black and white episodes that seemed far more fantasy than the cartoons on the next channel.

Patty's curly hair sat obediently on her shoulders. The dress hugged her hourglass figure, but not too tightly. Just enough to showcase those curves.

What captivated everyone here was her smile. It was brighter than the setting sun. That's probably why the sun was setting. Because it couldn't outshine her.

Whenever she came near, something always ballooned inside Grizz. A feeling he could never name, that he could never quite put his finger on. And always, like a needle seeking true north, he kept coming back around to be in her presence.

She'd blossomed from the girl in cutoffs and pigtails to become the Homecoming Queen and the Prom Queen. She'd even won a beauty competition a year ago. In the high school yearbook, she was voted Most Liked.

Everybody liked Patty Keaton. What was not to like about her? Nothing.

Except that she was Keaton's baby sister, and Grizz had known her since she was in diapers.

True, he'd been in kindergarten at the time. When his new friend, Keaton, had brought Grizz into his quaint little cul-de-sac after school one day, Grizz had peered into the playpen and saw a bundle of red hair and pink cheeks. The little one who had gripped his finger had fascinated him.

Grizz made daily visits to the Keaton household. Each time, he'd peek into the playpen. He liked watching little Patty Keaton in her sleep. He liked talking to the growing toddler as she babbled on and making her smile. While Keaton had wanted to play soldiers, Grizz had preferred to read to the little girl who listened with rapt attention as he told Dr.

Seuss's stories. Patty would smile and grin up at him like he was her hero.

Right now, she was smiling and grinning at some other guy as she walked right past Grizz.

"Mac," said Patty. "You made it."

"Hey, Patty Cakes." Mac swooped her up in a bear hug, lifting her off the ground so that her dress twirled about her long, lean legs.

Grizz wanted to growl. Partly because Mac had her in his arms. Mostly because Mac had dared to call her by Grizz's pet name for her. Grizz had known Patty for her whole life. In the past, he'd always been the first one she ran to. He'd always gotten her grins and smiles.

Mac hardly knew her. He didn't know that she didn't have a sweet tooth and put cinnamon in her tea. He didn't know that she still slept with a stuffed giraffe named Jemmy instead of a teddy bear. Or that she had a smile that made Grizz believe he could wrestle down a bear.

"The Army's been good to you." Patty felt at Mac's biceps. "Look how big your muscles have gotten."

Mac preened under her attention and flexed. Patty's grin widened, showing off that brilliant light in her crystal-blue eyes. The light that turned on when she was up to mischief.

Still, knowing she was up to something, didn't temper Grizz's mood.

"He has a girlfriend," Grizz growled from behind them.

Patty turned her head and looked over her shoulder. Her dazzling eyes came to rest upon Grizz's face. Finally. And there was that ballooning feeling inside of him, pulling him toward her like she was the doorway to home after a long day of work.

"Hey, Grizzly Bear."

"Patricia."

Patty frowned. Using her full name was like pulling her pigtails. Which he hadn't done in years because she no longer wore her curls in pigtails. She no longer wore cutoff jeans and scuffed sneakers like the tomboy she'd used to be.

Patricia Keaton was a tomboy no longer. She wasn't a kid any longer. She was eighteen. A woman grown.

A slow smile spread across her face. Gone was the baby fat in her cheeks. Her high cheekbones were sharp angles that young men started doing acrobatics for. Her once gangly limbs now went on for days, ending in strappy shoes that would likely give normal men a foot fetish.

"Well, I knew you'd make it to my party, Grizz. I can always count on you."

Grizz's gaze slid back to that smile. He'd made her giggle as a kid. He'd delighted her when he'd pushed her on a swing set. She'd grinned up at him as he'd read her the silly poems he'd loved so much as a kid. She'd smiled politely, if uncomprehending, as he'd tried to explain the more complicated poems he enjoyed as a young man.

Patty was the only girl he could spend long afternoons with and not feel the need to rush away. He'd never felt the pressure to be anything more than what he was with her. Likely because they'd known each other so long.

"What about your big brother?" said Keaton. "Am I chopped liver over here?"

"I happen to like chopped liver," she said.

"Because you're weird," said Keaton.

Keaton poked her in the shoulder. Patty ducked and smacked at his hand. The two tussled; Keaton in his sturdy army boots, Patty in her delicate sandals.

She'd had to learn to defend herself as the only girl in a house with a military father, a brother who was aimed for the same path, and Grizz, who didn't understand that girls shouldn't learn how to box. Patty, even in a dress and heels, could hold her own.

At that moment, Grizz saw the girl she used to be. The one he could wrestle with out in the backyard. The one he'd spent quiet Friday nights with watching a marathon of the *Andy Griffith Show* or *Happy Days*. The one he didn't have to think twice about when she rested her head against his shoulder.

Keaton feinted right. Patty had the space to sneak in for a strike. Instead, she stepped back and fell into Grizz. He caught her, bringing her lush body into his. All the fight went out of her. The resistance went out of him as well.

It had been a long time since Grizz had touched Patty. Years since they'd sat close together on a couch while she'd rested her head on his shoulder. This was why.

Grizz's gaze dipped to Patty's mouth. Patty parted her lips. Her pink tongue darted out as she wet those lips. Grizz's hold tightened on her. Everything inside him screaming one single word.

Mine.

"Ha!" shouted Keaton. "Gotcha. Hold her Grizz."

Yes. That's exactly what he wanted to do. Hold Patty tight and never let her go. Tuck her head against his chest so that she could feel how his heart pounded for her. Lift her chin to watch her wet her lips again and then claim her mouth.

Grizz let Patty go. His arms straightened as he shoved her away. Patty wobbled on unsteady feet, and Grizz had to stop himself from reaching for her again.

When his gaze met hers, gone was the brightness in her eyes. The glittering azure had faded into smudges of a blue that could've almost been called gray. Patty stepped away, rejection in her gaze. She gave them all a curt nod and then walked away.

"Why'd you let her go?" Keaton gave him a shove.

The blow from his best friend was light. Grizz's whole body canted to the side like he might fall over from the light tap. He'd just released the one and only thing in the world he wanted desperately but couldn't have. He'd just let go of his best friend's little sister.

"I see you understand me about The One." Mac clapped Grizz on the back. "You are so screwed."

Grizz was so screwed. He had the hots for Patricia Keaton. Mac may have figured it out. Grizz just hoped he could hide his feelings well enough so that his best friend never found out.

CHAPTER TWO

*P*atty was going to kill her brother. It didn't matter that he was the best big brother a girl could ever ask for. Keaton never tattled on her. Especially when she didn't eat her veggies. Instead, he'd shown her how to sneak them into the trash when they were sitting at the dinner table, and their parents' backs were turned.

Keaton often let Patty tag along with him and his friends. Mainly because no one ever thought his pack of friends could be up to no good if Keaton's little sister was with them. They were often wrong.

Whenever Patty was up to no good with her own pack of friends, Keaton often wanted in on whatever she'd plotted, certain he could make the plan better. He was usually right about making her plans better.

There was just one plan she'd never let Keaton in on. It was the plan that would determine the course of her life. That was Patty's plan to marry her brother's best friend.

Patricia Keaton was used to getting her way. From a very early age, she knew she possessed the main attributes to get what she wanted in life. With her small hands, she'd felt her chubby cheeks after having them pinched and patted so often as a child. She'd looked in a mirror and stretched her lips wide, trying to see what others saw in her gap-toothed grin. She'd stared in her blue eyes and tried to see the sparkle her mother's friends insisted was there. She didn't see any of it, but she understood that others did and that that gave her an advantage.

Except when it came to Grizz.

Grizz wasn't immune to Patty's charms. He spent a lot of time trying to make her smile. She knew that her giggle brought about his chuckles. She knew that she could hold his attention if she stared into his eyes.

Patty knew Grizz liked her. Just not in the way she liked him. Because she didn't like Grizz. She loved him.

She'd known she'd loved him since her mother

had taught her the word. As a child, Patty loved her mother. She loved her father. She loved her brother.

Those same warm and fuzzy feelings were there for Grizz. But they were somehow different, more. Since Patty had learned the word love and learned his name, she knew that Grizz and love belonged in the same sentence together.

From that day forward, she'd decided to learn everything about him. She knew his favorite television shows; he loved the black and white classics like *Leave it to Beaver* and *The Andy Griffith Show* that showcased a simpler time. He loved poetry, from the simple stuff like Dr. Seuss to the complex lyrical stylings of Byron, which she could never wrap her head around. She knew he loved his meat with just a touch of fire like her. But unlike her, Grizz liked a side of vegetables. Even with that flaw, she loved him still and knew they could make it work.

Patty had been hoping that tonight, at her graduation party, Grizz would finally see in her everything she wanted him to see. She'd worn the perfect fifties dress. Her hair was coiled in a bun like Donna Reed. She'd even worn pearls. She was the perfect representation of his perfect wife.

And then her brother had gone and ruined everything.

"Patty, don't be like that," Keaton called after her as she stormed away from their group.

Keaton had always treated her as an equal. Which meant that sometimes he forgot she was a girl. She had never been helpless in a conflict or skittish at the sight of bugs like many of her girlfriends who cried if they got a speck of dirt on their clothing. Patty Keaton could hold her own, be it boy, bug, or beast.

But tonight, she didn't want to be seen as her brother's equal. She wanted to be seen as Grizz's. Maybe that was the problem? A proper girl wouldn't have struck back. She would've retreated.

Even though it rankled, Patty knew what she had to do. She slowed her retreat and let Keaton catch up to her. The moment he caught her, Patty twisted the heel of her shoe and yelped.

"Ouch."

She let her body fall to the ground, making sure to arrange her limbs gracefully as she landed. The party came to a screeching halt. All eyes were on her, but she only cared about the dark eyes looming toward her.

"Keaton," growled Grizz. "What did you do?"

"Nothing." Keaton held up his hands, innocent for once in his life. "I didn't touch her."

Grizz shoved Keaton out of the way. "Careful."

"She's faking it," said Keaton.

Patty faked a sniffle at her faux injury. It was a command performance. One that she was rewarded for when Grizz lifted her up into his arms.

Patty wrapped her arms around Grizz's neck as he turned and headed for the house. With Grizz's focus on the backdoor and his back turned to his friends, Patty couldn't resist. She stuck her tongue out at her brother.

Before Keaton could retaliate, the back door slammed closed. The house was empty. Her mother was across the street at a neighbor's house, secure in the knowledge that nothing would go wrong while Keaton and his friends were watching over the new high school graduates.

Holly Keaton wasn't stupid. She knew that if there was any trouble, her two kids would likely be in the lead of the melee. She also knew that as long as Griffin Hayes was silently watching over the Keaton kids that she had a spy in their midst.

Grizz respected their mom more than he did his own mom. Probably because Amanda Hayes was rarely home, hadn't set a warm meal on the table in years, and taught Grizz how to forge her signature for school documents soon after he learned cursive writing so she didn't have to deal with backpack mail. Grizz had been his own parent for years. The only time he got a break was when he came over to their house where he could get a warm meal out of the oven, a scolding to behave, and a hug before he went home to bed.

Grizz sat Patty on the table. She was reluctant to unfold her arms from around his strong torso. But she did so as he bent down on his knee. This was how she imagined him proposing. But instead of taking her left hand, he took her right ankle and examined it.

"It doesn't look like you broke any skin," he said.

"Can you get me an ice pack?"

Grizz went to the fridge. He pulled the door opened and examined the contents like he owned this place. He'd practically lived here since he was eight, and she was five. Her earliest memories were of him.

When Grizz put the ice pack on her ankle, she hissed. His gaze shot to hers, concern rimming his hazel eyes. That hazel gaze dipped to her lips.

And there it was, proof that he wanted her. Guys always looked at her lips when she talked. The older she got, she knew it wasn't her dimpled grin they were interested in. But Patty had never wanted any boy's lips near hers. She was eighteen and had never been kissed. Because she was saving that honor for the man in front of her.

"Just keep this here," said Grizz, preparing to rise. "I should—"

Patty gripped his hand to hold him in place. He was stronger than her, so he could've moved if he wanted to. He held still. But he averted his gaze.

"Thanks for coming to my party, Grizz."

"Of course, I'm here. Why wouldn't I be?"

"Because things have been weird between us."

Before he'd left for the service, things had been normal between them. The last time they'd hung out was a year ago. They'd curled up on the couch to watch a marathon of *The Patty Duke Show*. One of her favorites, and not just because of her namesake. She loved the twin cousins where one was refined and the other more adventurous. They reminded her so much of herself, especially since it was the same actress playing both roles. She'd leaned into Grizz like she'd done many times as a kid, but for some reason, that night, he stiffened and pulled away from her. He made some excuse about being home in time to see his mom and then darted out of the house.

They hadn't been alone again since.

Grizz didn't respond to her for a long moment. "I wouldn't miss your party for the world. You're practically my little sister."

Patty lowered her head. Her finger pads pressed into the wood of the table as she tried to hold herself together and not pout or shout like she would've only a few years ago when she didn't get her way. She might always be Keaton's little sister, but she was grown now and determined to act it.

Starting now. What happened on the other side of the back door to get her in here alone with Grizz didn't count.

"You're off to college soon," Grizz continued.

That was a topic Patty didn't wish to discuss. She had no desire to go to college. The only degree she wanted was an MRS. She'd been studying at the school of Hayes all her life, and she was ready for the final exam, the one that got her the full time, lifelong job as Mrs. Griffin Hayes.

"You're going to have a lot of new experiences," Grizz went on. "New friends. College boys."

"I won't be busy with college boys," Patty said. "There's only ever been one boy that I wanted."

Grizz pulled away from her. Patty hopped to her feet, all pretense of an injured ankle gone. She was not letting him get away again. Especially not when he was leaving again for training. She was perfectly fine with having a long-distance relationship with him. The key was to get that relationship started. She'd waited all her life to be able to tell him how she felt and have him take her seriously. That time was now.

"Grizz, I think you know how I feel about you."

Grizz shook his head. Patty got the sense that he wasn't denying her words. His gaze appeared as though it were turned inward like he was denying a voice inside his own head.

"Patricia, this cannot happen."

"What's wrong with me?" She couldn't help it. Patty's lower lip trembled.

Grizz's haunted gaze lifted to her, followed by hands that cupped her face. "Nothing. You're perfect."

"Then, why not?" Patty stomped her foot, all pretext of being grown gone. She'd smiled and grinned and gotten all dressed up and worn these uncomfortable shoes. What more was she supposed to do?

Grizz raised an eyebrow at her. Then he sighed. "You're my best friend's sister."

"Then dump Keaton. He's been holding you back."

Grizz tried biting his lip, but that didn't work. A chuckle escaped his perfectly formed lips. There was a hint of stubble there despite the shaving regiment he now put himself through as a member of the United States Armed Services. He'd always been hairy, like a life-sized teddy bear.

"You know Keaton wants what's best for me," said Patty. "Seems to me that that would be his best friend."

"That's cute." Grizz gave her cheek a pinch. Before he could let her face go, Patty cupped his hand with hers, keeping him there.

Grizz shook his head at her, resignation darkened his gaze. He could've pulled away from her hold. He was stronger than her. But he didn't. He ran his thumb across the top of her cheek as he said the words that would break her heart.

"This is not going to happen, Patty Cakes. You're going to go to college, get your degree, meet a nice boy."

"A nice boy? You really want me to break some poor little boy in two?"

She got another one of Grizz's grins for that truthful statement.

"You're the only one who's ever been able to handle me. I'm destined to be Mrs. Griffin Hayes. Have your babies. Be in your bed."

Again his gaze dipped to her lips. She could taste his breath. He gulped, as though trying to swallow down his desire, but hunger remained in his darkened gaze.

As if it had a mind of its own, Grizz's thumb brushed at her bottom lip. As though it was testing what his mouth wanted most. The pad of his finger was rough on her untouched flesh.

Patty parted her lips, ready to beg for him to take her. She knew that if he kissed her then, it would seal the deal. She was so close to having it all.

Grizz exhaled. The small release of air appeared to weigh him down, making his face sink closer to hers. He was close enough for his chest to brush against hers. Inside her heart, Patty heard the gears shifting into place, making room to align perfectly with the man she knew she was destined to spend the rest of her life with.

"Patty?"

They both turned at the sound of Keaton's voice coming from the other room. Patty had no idea why her brother had chosen to come through the front door instead of the back one.

"Mom called from Mrs. Jenkins. She saw what happened and says I have to say I'm sorry. Even though you slipped on your own."

Their mother had eyes in the back of her head. Of course, she saw what had happened between her children. The question was, could she also see what was about to happen between Patty and Grizz?

Patty would not find out. When she turned back, Grizz had evaded her. He slipped out the back door. The last thing she heard was the quiet slap of the door. And then he was gone.

CHAPTER THREE

resent Day

"You're just going to stand there and let this happen to your blood?"

Grizz's lips curled in disgust at the words hurled into the late afternoon air. The words weren't aimed at Grizz, but he felt their impact. Grizz's gaze connected with Angel Bautista. The young man was the unfortunate recipient of the accusation.

Angel's lip curled in revulsion as he turned his back on his uncle. His fists tightened, and a crackling sound emitted from his palms. Brown shells fell to the ground as Angel popped a raw peanut into his mouth.

Manuel Bautista struggled against his handcuffs as he shouted at his nephew. "You're a disgrace to your family."

"No, Uncle," Angel called over his shoulder without turning to meet his uncle's gaze, "that was you."

Just before dawn, Manuel, a former hand of the Vance ranch, had decided his severance package would be the new calves that had been separated for branding. Luckily, before Manuel could get the herd of calves into the No Man's Land that lay beyond the borders of The Purple Heart Ranch and Vance Ranch, Grizz and his Army Ranger brothers had run him down and caught the thief.

Angel, who had remained loyal to the Vances, had helped hunt his wayward uncle down. Now, the young man walked away from his former mentor, severing the last tie.

"Where do you think you're going, Angel?"

The younger Bautista did turn back at the sound of the deputy sheriff's voice. It wasn't that Deputy Newman's voice rang with authority. It rankled with undue self-importance.

"You're still needed for questioning in this here

investigation, boy." The deputy slammed the door with his first quarry inside, then rounded the squad car, gaze intent on new prey.

Angel didn't step back as Newman advanced. He held his ground, his dark head high. But behind his back, Grizz saw the young man's fists clench and release as though he were searching for deliverance. Instead of deliverance, he crunched more shells and was rewarded with another handful of peanuts.

It was the deputy who stepped back. Newman's body coiled away from Angel. His features contorted in horror.

"I'm allergic to those." Newman pointed at the shells surrounding Angel's boots.

"Ah, my bad. I didn't know." Angel's voice rang with false apology.

Grizz failed to hide his grin at the young man. Grizz knew what it was to have a family member's shortcomings projected on to himself, even though he'd never put one foot out of place. The same was happening now to Angel.

"We've already told you Angel's part in the matter," Grizz spoke up. "He helped track down Mr. Bautista and recovered the stolen property."

"Yeah, but it's people like him that we have to

watch out for." The deputy leaned into Grizz as though the two were in cahoots.

Grizz leaned away from the man in distaste.

"How do I know the two of them weren't in on it to begin with?" sneered Newman.

"Because we all vouched for him." Grizz waved his hand at the other soldiers helping Brenda lead the weary calves into a pasture in the distance.

Newman's lips pinched. He looked from Grizz to Angel, to the shells on the ground, and then back to Angel. "Don't leave town."

With that edict, the deputy turned on his booted heel and rounded the car to the driver's side. Manuel Bautista glared out of the side window until the engine turned over, and the car pulled off. When Grizz turned back, Angel was gone.

As he watched the elder Bautista being carted away, he felt a twinge of sympathy for the old man. Grizz knew what it was like to reach higher than his station. To want something he had no right to. But unlike the old man, Grizz would never take what was not his.

That was pretty much the story of his life. Even joining the elite Army Ranger force had not shaken the stank of his lower-class breeding from his back.

The stank wasn't the only thing from his past that was clinging to him. The poverty was back.

Grizz had sent nearly all of his money earned from the army back home to his mother to pay off his father's debts. After twenty years, his mother was finally free and clear of the mess Malcolm Hayes had buried them under. But that had left Grizz without enough to pay his fair share for the new Army Ranger Training Camp he and his friends were building.

Grizz knew Keaton would front him the money. His best friend always had his back since they were kids. But Grizz hated handouts. He always insisted on earning his own way. Being an equal member and investor in this venture was his dream. But like the other things he'd dreamed he could have in his life, this one too might stay out of his reach.

"Hey, Grizzly Bear."

The voice came from behind him. He had learned not to have his back to the enemy. She wasn't the enemy. But she was the greatest danger to him.

Grizz turned to find a young woman standing behind him. All five-foot-four inches and one-hundred-ten pounds of her. Bright blue eyes filled with intelligence and mischief—a lethal combination. Flaming red hair that rivaled a blaze, a warning not to touch. As if he needed a warning to keep his hands off his best friend's sister.

"What are you doing here, Patty Cakes?" he said.

"I came to meet my new sister-in-law and see my two favorite guys," Patty said.

He hadn't seen her in three years. The Keaton household had not been a second home to him, it had been his dream home. But that door closed when he'd nearly kissed Patty on the night of her graduation.

She'd been a vision that night. She'd taunted his desires. Tested his control. He'd nearly broken when he had her in his arms in the kitchen. And then Keaton had walked in.

If his best friend had seen Grizz with his baby sister in his arms, ready to taste the impish grin that had always fascinated him, Keaton would've banished him from not only his home but his life. And Grizz would've deserved it for even thinking the thought of laying a claim on Patty.

"Don't I get a hug?"

A hug was dangerous. A hug meant that she'd be in his arms. She wasn't all gangly limbs anymore. Patty had even more curves now than the last time he'd seen her. Those curves were headed straight for him.

Grizz took a step back, but it was too late. She was on him. She wrapped her arms around his neck like she would put him in a submission hold. Because he could never say no to her.

Except for the night when she had asked him to give her her first kiss. He'd told her no. But inside, Grizz had felt a growl rise from his gut into his throat.

Mine, that primal beast wanted to shout then.

Mine, it wanted to howl now that the woman who fit him perfectly was back in his arms where she belonged.

Grizz ducked away from Patty's hold. In the distance, he saw Keaton headed for them. With his background, Grizz knew he wasn't the guy for a girl like Patty. And with the uncertainty of his financial future, he knew he would never be.

"Patty Cakes? Is that you?"

Patty dragged her gaze from Grizz to her brother. Keaton opened his arms, and she went into them. Introductions were made with Keaton's wife of a few days, Brenda. While that happened, Grizz allowed himself to finally take her in.

He'd made a deal with himself; he could think

about her so long as he didn't see her. And oh, man, had he thought about her over the years. Holding her, kissing her, sometimes just looking into her eyes. Patty had always looked at him like he was a hero. But what kind of hero would go after his best friend's little sister? It would be the height of betrayal. It would be something Grizz's father would do.

"Shouldn't you be in school?" said Keaton.

"Spring break," said Patty.

But there was a hitch to her voice. She wasn't telling the whole story.

"That's a week, right?" said Brenda, excitement rising in her voice. "You'll stay the week with us?"

Grizz wanted to protest. A whole week of avoiding Patty? He would not survive.

Patty's gaze found his. Mischief shone through. "If it's not too much trouble."

Oh, it was trouble. It was far too much trouble. A week with Patty Keaton was going to be filled with nothing but trouble.

CHAPTER FOUR

*P*atty had always wanted a sister. Brenda was a bit unexpected. She drove a tractor, corralled bulls, and rode horses. The tomboy in Patty screamed to slip on a pair of worn jeans, saddle up, and let her hair fly behind her as she rode through the pastures shouting giddy-up.

Taking in a deep breath, Patty exhaled the thought. She was no longer that wild child. She was a grown woman. A sophisticated, refined, grown woman who would make a soldier a perfect wife. If said soldier stayed around to pay her any mind.

It had been three years since she'd seen Grizz. Three. During that time, she'd caught glimpses of him as she video chatted with Keaton. But Grizz never held still for the camera, often giving her a quick wave, and then excusing himself from anymore face time with her.

Grizz didn't come home for holidays either. Instead, he stayed on base while Keaton came home for visits. Grizz made it a point to visit during the offseason, times when she would be knee-deep in exams and finals. It was like he was purposely avoiding her.

"This here was my prize bull," Brenda was saying.

Patty's attention jerked to the present moment. A large animal swaggered over to where they stood at the fence. The bull was an imposing beast. With its thick legs and broad back. Its nostrils flared as it regarded Patty. A proper lady would've run away at the massive animal's approach.

Patty's gaze connected with the bull. There was a softness to its dark eyes. A weariness about its approach that said *I could hurt you if I wanted to*. Patty knew the bull had no intention of hurting her. She reached out her hand to its horns.

"Careful," admonished Brenda.

But her new sister-in-law was too late. The bull had already bowed its head to allow for Patty's touch. Its hairy head was matted with coarse curls. It huffed out a puff of air that sounded much to Patty's ears as a sign of resignation. She'd heard tired puppies make the same noise.

"Great," sighed Brenda. "He might as well be castrated."

"What do you mean?" said Patty as she scratched at the animal's head.

"This bull was meant to party with all the girls if you know what I'm saying," said Brenda. "But he got into a fight with your brother, and now he's completely out of commission."

"He looks fine to me."

"He's supposed to be a raging bull, ready for business. He should not be letting you pet his head."

"Well, I have a way with big beasts."

Patty's gaze tracked across the field where her brother, Mac, and Grizz were lifting bales of hay. Patty's gaze caught and held on the flex of Grizz's muscles under his damp t-shirt.

Brenda followed the trajectory of Patty's gaze and grinned. "I'll bet you do."

Actually, she didn't.

For the rest of the night, Grizz avoided being alone with Patty. He'd sat as far away from her as possible last night at dinner. He turned in to bed early while the rest of them stayed up to play board games. In the morning, he was out of the house before the sun rose.

Grizz spent the morning out in the barns with the animals. Then he disappeared with the guys over to their training camp around lunchtime. By then, Patty had been on the ranch for over twenty-four hours, and she hadn't spoken any more words to Grizz than that first meeting. Things were not going according to her plan.

It was an old plan, a simple plan. Altered only slightly because she knew that Grizz felt something for her. Confirmed by the way he avoided her at every turn.

Patty's plan was to get Grizz to acknowledge his feelings for her. To do that, she needed to corner him and finish the business they'd started three years ago at her graduation party. She knew that if she got Grizz to give her her first kiss, it would seal the deal on their future happiness.

Turning on her cellphone, Patty checked her email and saw a number of missives from teachers at her school. There were emails about missing assignments. Other notes asked where she was during this exam period. Three emails were from the dean about her failing grades.

Patty deleted them all. They were no longer

relevant. Just like school wasn't relevant. Patty had gotten her priorities straight. That's why she was here. She'd wasted three years on a degree she had no use for. Now she was back on track for the only certificate she ever wanted, the one that gave her her MRS.

And now those three letters were again within her reach. The moment she'd known that her brother and his friends were retiring, Patty had started hatching her plan. When she'd learned their location, she got in her car and started driving across the country.

And now she was here. On a ranch. In a kitchen. Unsure of what to do next.

"You must be Patricia."

Patty turned to see a tall man standing in the doorway. The man had what her mother would call a trusting face. His features were relaxed, his smile certain of his place in the world. But there was something mischievous in the lift of his green eyes.

"And you are?" asked Patty.

That grin widened, and he winked one green eye. "I'm your new brother. I'm Brenda's brother. Pastor Vance. But you can call me Walter."

Patty's own grin faltered at the title he put before his name. "Wait? You're a real live priest?"

"I hope so." Walter tugged at his collar, his grin still in place. "Otherwise, your brother and my sister's marriage is a fake."

"You married them?"

"Sure did. They came into the courthouse, marriage license in one hand, prenup in the other."

"Surprisingly, that does sound like my brother."

A prenup might not sound very romantic. But Patty knew that Keaton would've wanted to have a plan and contingencies for his future life in place. She was also willing to bet that the agreement left Brenda with everything if the marriage were to dissolve.

"The two got married to save this ranch and further your brother's grand camp idea," Walter continued.

He'd made his way to the refrigerator and was pulling out vegetables. Carrots, broccoli, and a bushel of leafy greens that made Patty's stomach turn a paler shade of green.

"Though I don't think they appreciate that story any longer. They've basically rewritten their love story as it was love at first sight and not because a bull ran into Keaton's car."

Walter chuckled as he began chopping the rabbit

food. Unfortunately, he hadn't pulled out any rabbit meat.

"Too bad for them, I know the real deal. Otherwise, it'd be their word against mine, and they could try and claim spousal privilege."

"Spousal privilege?" asked Patty.

"You know, that law where you can't make a husband and wife testify against each other."

Walter tossed the minced garden scraps into a pan and sprinkled spices. But even the warm herbal scent couldn't entice Patty to consider eating the colorful food. When Walter next emerged from the fridge, he had a steak redder than her lipstick. Now, they were talking.

"Happens more often than you'd think out here," said Walter.

"What?" asked Patty, her eyes on the meat cooking a tad too long in the hot pan for her tastes. "Spousal privilege?"

"Marriage of conveniences. Couples turn up here, and before you know it, they're saying their I do's. The ranch next door is filled with soldiers who've gotten married within months, some within days of arriving here."

"Really?" Patty said as she glanced out the window at one soldier riding atop a horse. Grizz's bearded face was hairier than the animal upon whose back he rode.

"But no need to worry," said Walter. "Your brother tells me your just here for the week before you head back to school."

"Right."

Patty couldn't help but glance back out the window. But this time she looked up in the sky, searching for any sign of lightning. Wasn't lightning supposed to strike if you lied to a priest?

CHAPTER FIVE

*G*rizz hadn't slept a wink for the last two nights. He'd spent only a week here in one of Brenda's spare bedrooms, but in that time, he'd learned every creak, every groan, every sigh of the old homestead.

There was only silence in the house at three in the morning. But Grizz swore he heard her every shift beneath the covers, her every exhale as she dreamed. What was his Patty Cakes dreaming of? Did his face appear in her head as he tried in vain to rest as hers did in his?

Every night for the past three years, he'd dreamed of Patricia Keaton. Smiling at him. Laughing with him. Sitting beside him and resting her head against his shoulder, something she'd done countless times before. But on that fateful night at her graduation party, Grizz had come to the startling realization that his Patty Cakes was no longer the child he adored, but the woman he desired.

Now, she lay in the room across the hall from him, unguarded, unprotected against those same desires that were still inside of him. Two flimsy pieces of wood and less than twenty steps were all that separated them. This had been much easier when he could keep an ocean between them.

Grizz scrubbed his hands over his face. He pulled at the thick hair on his chin, trying to get his mind right. Barely two days had passed.

How was he going to get to the end of her spring break week without accidentally brushing his fingers against hers and then pulling her to him? Or focusing on her lips as she spoke only to unwittingly find his own mouth pressed against hers? And there was always the threat that she would stand before him and repeat the words she'd said when she first got here; *Don't I get a hug?*

Grizz knew that if she came back into his arms again, he would not let her go.

She'd had three years to get over her little crush on him. Three years to date other boys her own age. Surely, she'd forgotten her feelings for him. But he couldn't take the chance in case she still harbored any thought of the two of them together.

After years of fighting to protect his country, Grizz was weary of combat. He'd grown tired of traveling and tossing and turning on a different mattress each night. He craved any semblance of normalcy. But, he knew that normal could not include an intimate relationship with his best friend's sister.

Grizz dragged his weary, unrested body out of bed while the moon was high, and the sun was still nestled under the cover of the dark sky. He slipped on a fresh shirt and jeans and stepped into his boots.

He knew Patty never rose early. When he'd slept over as a child, Mrs. Keaton would send him into her room to wake her. Patty was prone to kick and punch if roused before she was ready.

He'd never minded her kicks and punches. They didn't hurt. He caught them easily, then tickled her awake. She always woke with a smile for him, eyes shining bright.

Grizz had loved her giggles. He'd loved her smiles. He loved it when she opened those big blue eyes. He never felt more at peace than when she was looking up at him.

Those blue eyes met him as he opened his door.

Her hair was tousled from the pillows. She wore a long nightgown that did nothing to hide the fact that she was now a woman and no longer a child. But what Grizz couldn't take his eyes off of were her pink toes peeking out from beneath her cotton gown.

"Morning," she said.

Grizz's eyes snapped back up to her face. "You should be in bed."

"But I'm wide awake."

"It's three in the morning, Patty. Go back to bed."

Her right brow lifted as the left side of her mouth curled into an amused grin. Grizz was fascinated by the asymmetry of it.

"I'm not a child, Griffin. You can't tell me when to go to bed. Unless you want to come and tuck me in."

Patty took a few steps toward him. Her bare feet padded silently on the floorboards. Grizz felt he was under attack, but something in him would not let him retreat. It took all his willpower to keep his hands at his sides and not reach for her.

She stopped when she was a foot away from him. Her head cocked to the side, like an inquisitive, little bird. If he bent his head down, he could nuzzle against her neck like he'd seen actual love birds do.

"Are you mad at me?"

Grizz's head jerked back, as though she'd slapped him. "No, of course not."

"Then why won't you talk to me?"

"I'm talking to you now."

"We used to be so close, and now you run anytime I come near you."

Grizz opened his mouth, but none of the false, placating words would pass his lips.

Patty's hands rose. His gaze followed them like they were heat-seeking missiles that had locked on their targets. There was no escape. When her soft, warm palms landed on his chest Grizz felt his heart explode inside his chest. He was left in tattered pieces at the slightest touch of her.

"I missed you," she whispered. Her face tilted up. Her blue eyes shone so big, so bright in her perfectly round face.

Just like when they were kids, Grizz felt himself wrapped around her baby finger. He was prepared to indulge her in any whim. To give her her heart's desire. The problem was, he knew what she wanted, and it was the one thing he had to deny her.

Grizz covered his hands with hers. His rough skin burned as it enveloped her soft flesh. "This cannot happen between us, Patty."

"But you want it to, don't you?"

How had their fingers become entwined? It was not what he intended. He had to break away from her. But he couldn't unravel his digits from the sturdy lacing. Her pinky finger rested heavy against one of his knuckles like it was the key turned into an unyielding lock.

"No," Grizz tried, but his voice was choked.

Patty's smile was slow, even a little wicked as she continued to gaze up at him with guileless eyes. "You've never lied to me before."

Grizz exhaled through his nose. But he needed air to fill his lungs so he could think, so he could speak. The problem was, when he inhaled, all he smelled was the sweet scent of Patricia Keaton. A scent that had haunted and taunted him for three years.

"You know I've loved you my whole life," Patty continued.

"Patty Cakes," he sighed, pulling forth the last ounce of his willpower to get the words out. "It's just a crush."

"It is not."

Patty stomped her foot. Her beautiful face contorted in a fury he hadn't seen since she was an adolescent told by her mother that it was bedtime.

Footsteps sounded at the end of the hall. The

knob of a door rattled. It was the door of the master bedroom where Brenda and Keaton slept.

Grizz yanked his hands from Patty's and stepped back just as the door opened.

"What's going on out here?" asked Keaton. His gaze was unfocused from sleep.

"Just a little fight over the bathroom," Grizz called over his shoulder as he made his way down the stairs. "I'll use the downstairs one."

Grizz raced down the stairs, uncaring of his booming footfalls. It would be better to wake the whole house than to be alone one more second with Patty confessing the words he didn't allow himself to dream of.

Her feelings hadn't changed. She still wanted him. He wanted her.

He hadn't said it out loud, couldn't. But he had missed her these last few years. There had been a Patty-sized hole in his life.

Grizz ran his hands over his face. He came away with dirt from the mud at the campgrounds. Fitting because that's who he was, a dirty old man at twenty-five lusting after the little girl he'd once known.

But she's not a little girl anymore, insisted the voice in his head. *She's a full-grown woman who wants you.*

Oh, yeah, thought Grizz. Who's going to tell that to her big brother?

"You're up early," said Keaton.

Grizz dropped the tools in his hands and spun around. He hadn't even heard Keaton drive up to the training campground. Grizz had been so consumed with trying not to think about Patty that he clearly wasn't thinking about anything else either.

"Hey," said Keaton, "what's going on with you and my sister?"

"What? Nothing. Why would you say that?"

Keaton paused, a chainsaw in his hand as he turned to face his best friend. "I don't know? The two of you seem different when you're together?"

Keaton checked the blades of the tool. He hit the ON switch, and the spinning blades roared to life. He shut off the device and looked expectantly at Grizz.

"Come to think of it," said Keaton as he sat the chainsaw down, "I haven't seen you two together in the last two days at all. Are you fighting?"

"What would we have to fight about? We haven't seen each other in years."

"Yeah," Keaton frowned. "It has seemed like the two of you have grown apart. That's too bad."

"It is?" Maybe Keaton wasn't as averse to his best friend and his sister having a relationship after all?

"Something's definitely going on with her." Keaton picked up a shovel and came alongside Grizz. "Why would she choose to spend her spring break on a ranch and not on some beach with her friends? I think some jerk broke her heart, and she's running away. We'll get it out of her and then go wring the jerk's neck. Yeah?"

Keaton clapped Grizz on the back. The force of the impact wasn't hard, but it made Grizz's teeth rattle inside his head.

"Yeah," said Grizz. "Sounds good."

CHAPTER SIX

"That's a nice shirt you're wearing."

"Thanks." Patty gave a wane smile to the guy who'd sidled up to the bar next to her. Her mother had raised her to have manners, even when she didn't feel like using them. Like now.

After their encounter in the hall early in the morning, Grizz had avoided her for the rest of the day. To pass the time, Patty had helped Brenda with tagging the new calves while she and her ranch hand, Angel, had branded and castrated them. Both Brenda and Angel had worried over Patty after the first sizzle of burned flesh. Patty hadn't flinched.

She'd never been a squeamish kinda girl. In fact, she'd enjoyed getting her hands dirty and feeling useful. Something she hadn't felt in the last three years that she'd sat on hard chairs while a professor droned on, and Patty daydreamed about the life she truly wanted. A life beside Griffin Hayes.

"Can I check your tag?"

Patty's head whipped back to the guy leaning casually against the bar. She'd forgotten he was there. "I'm sorry, what?"

"Can I see your tag?" he repeated. "I want to check to see if it was made in heaven? Because someone as fine as you needs a parking ticket."

Patty tried and failed to hide her cringe. She'd heard some bad pickup lines during her time at frat parties. But at least those guys could stick with just one metaphor. She wondered if this guy knew what a metaphor was?

She was a little surprised that she remembered what the word meant since she hadn't paid much attention in English class in high school or her short-lived college career. Grizz had taught her about metaphors when he read her poetry. Most of Dr. Seuss's poetry involved metaphors. The Lorax was a metaphor of anger, and later in the story, hope. So was the Grinch. Patty had often wondered if Dr. Seuss was a depressed soul?

Those metaphorical references she got. Mainly because Grizz was the one explaining them to her, and she always hung on his every word. When her teachers in high school or college tried to cram other dead poets' words into her head, she lost the meaning, and her brain cells collided in an explosion.

Hmm? Was that a metaphor? Patty cocked her head to the side and met with dark eyes.

"I see you get me," said the guy—what was his name?

She hadn't gotten what he'd said or his name? But he thought she had. He apparently thought she was here for his pleasure.

She wasn't.

Patty was tracking another quarry. If she couldn't corral Grizz back at the ranch, then she'd catch him out of that habitat. The guys were due here any moment. Tonight Patty had every plan to tag Grizz as her own.

He couldn't refuse to dance with her if she asked him in front of the others. She knew that if she could just reclaim her old spot inside his arms, he would have no choice but to see her as the woman she was. Then there would be only one more step to her ultimate goal; for Grizz to brand her as his with a kiss.

Her first kiss. The kiss she should have had three years ago at her graduation party. She'd saved herself all these years, knowing that her heart would only ever belong to one person. And it wasn't the sleaze in front of her at the bar.

"Newman," he said as if she'd asked the question. "Deputy Sheriff Nick Newman."

"Patricia Keaton." Patty took his bony hand and shook. A shudder of displeasure went up her arm, and she quickly snatched her hand back.

She couldn't really blame the guy for approaching her. There weren't a lot of single people in the bar. There weren't really a lot of single people in the town.

Tonight the bar was filled with the residents of The Purple Heart Ranch. Patty had met the other men from the neighboring ranch. Each and every one of them here tonight had a ring on his finger. Pastor Vance hadn't been joking when he'd said that the soldiers at the Purple Heart Ranch came looking for healing and wound up married. Each one was more than happy to show pictures of his wife or kid or horse.

Patty liked each and every man and woman she

met from there. She wanted to be a part of the group and saw that they would welcome her. She was an army brat who had been blessed to live in the same place her whole life, but she could always easily fit in with anyone in the service. The people at the Purple Heart Ranch were her kinds of people. And she wanted to belong to their club in more ways than one.

The one and only path she planned to take to achieve that goal walked into the bar. Grizz didn't so much as walk as he swaggered. Every female gaze in the bar turned to check him out. Even a few of the wives. Patty knew they couldn't help it even though they were completely devoted to their husbands. Grizz just attracted the female gaze with his pure animal magnetism.

Patty leaned forward to get a better view of the man of her dreams. But she had to quickly jerk back as her nostrils filled with something distasteful. Deputy Sheriff Nick Newman's cologne cloyed her nose.

Didn't he know that a dab went a long way? Apparently not, since it appeared he'd doused himself with the whole bottle. Did he think the scent would attract women? It was having the opposite effect. It was more like woman-repellant.

Grizz's gaze swept the room. Patty knew when he saw her. She could feel the heat of his gaze fall on her cheeks. She didn't expect an encouraging smile from him. She wouldn't have been surprised at a small frown. But the hard glint of anger from his hazel eyes was a surprise.

"Tell me, Patricia Keaton, are you a religious woman? Because you've answered all my prayers."

Patty's stomach grumbled as the cop leaned in. From the corner of her eye, she saw Grizz angle his body toward them. The low hanging fruit would be to let this guy hit on her and make Grizz jealous. But she could never pull that off. Neither did she want to.

The only guy she wanted to flirt with was Grizz. The only guy she wanted to notice her was Grizz. He was noticing her now.

She was looking her best tonight. Since she'd turned eighteen and started on this quest to become Mrs. Griffin Hayes, Patty always made it a point to look her best. All her skirts were tailored. Each dress was only chosen if it flattered her curves, which she never tried to hide. She no longer owned a pair of sweats, not even the cute ones with fancy lettering on the backside. Her tomboy days were long over. If

Donna Reed or June Cleaver hadn't worn it, then neither did she.

Except jeans. She couldn't get by without a few pairs of jeans. Which is what she wore tonight. A fitted pair of jeans along with brand new cowboy boots.

Her makeup was done to accentuate her long lashes and eyes. Her lipstick was chosen to make men look at her lips. Which the guy in front of her was doing. But her lips were only for Grizz.

Countless men had looked at her lips, longingly. Not one had ever touched their lips to hers. She only wanted one man to do that, and he was stalking toward her now.

"Come on, angel, let's you and me get out of here." Deputy Newman's palm was hot, but his fingers were cold as they clamped around her forearm. It felt all wrong. But when she went to pull away, his fingers closed like a vise around her.

"You need to let the girl go." Grizz's voice was low. But even with the chatter of the bar, his growl was easily heard.

"What business is it of yours, Hayes?"

Grizz opened his mouth. Then he closed and pursed his lips.

"You got a claim on her or something?"

Grizz's throat worked another moment before he spoke. "She's my best friend's little sister. I helped raise her."

Fury clouded Patty's gaze. Would he never see her for the grown woman she was now? Would he never admit that he had feelings for her?

"Oh, your sister," said the cop. "Hope you don't mind me chatting with your little sister then. She's a nice piece."

Grizz's hazel gaze went as sharp as a shard of wood. But Newman didn't appear to notice. He was far too busy ogling Patty's chest.

"I'm sure you're fending guys off her all the time," Newman continued, still oblivious to the two-hundred-pound soldier who was very near a rage. "But I'm one of the good guys. I'm an officer of the law. She couldn't be in better hands."

"You hear that, Grizz?" Patty said through gritted teeth. "I couldn't be in better hands than his. Unless there was something you wanted to say to me? Maybe you wanted to say it somewhere private?"

"No," said Grizz, letting out a slow breath. "I just came over to check on you."

"Oh. How *brotherly* of you."

"That's what I'm here for."

"Well, you can run along now then."

Grizz held Patty's glare. In it, she knew he was telling her to be careful. She was done being careful. She was done being careless.

She was just done.

She watched Grizz walk off. She turned back to the bar and downed her drink. The virgin peanut butter cocktail gave her a sugar rush that went straight to her head. She wished she could be served something stronger, but she was only twenty. An adult, but without all the privileges of adulthood.

Patty decided she'd done enough adulting for the day. She was calling it a night. She grabbed her purse and headed for the door. Before she could cross the threshold, a hand grabbed her.

Once again, a shiver ran down her spine at the hot and cold of Deputy Sheriff Newman's fingers.

"Where do you think you're going?" he said.

"I'm going home."

"Sounds like a plan. I'll come, too."

"No, you're not invited." Patty stepped out of the bar and into the cool night air. The parking lot was filled with cars but empty of bodies.

"Do you think you can just walk away?"

"No," she said. "I brought my car."

Newman rounded her, planting himself between her and her car. "You led me on back there."

"No, I didn't. I was polite while you entertained yourself with cheesy come-ons."

"Girls like you make me sick." His lip curled, stripping away any hint of handsomeness.

"Girls like me? Seriously, has any woman ever fallen for any of that stuff you were saying? I'm doubting it. Listen, I wasn't being my authentic self back there with you, I admit it. But I also wasn't being an inappropriate jerk. Eyes up here, buddy."

His gaze snapped to hers. For a second. And then they were back on her chest. The guy was clearly a lost cause. It was not her responsibility to try and teach him manners, especially this late in life.

Patty turned to go. Once again, a cold-warm shock held her back.

"You're not going anywhere until I get what I want from you."

Patty turned slowly. More than a couple of times, she'd had to defend herself against a randy man who didn't know how to read the clear signals of a brush-off. Before she used her fists as her brother and Grizz taught her, she decided to give this jerk one last try and use her words.

"I gave you no signals. I'm now clearly stating that I have no interest in you. And here again, I'm going to use my manners and say no and thank you. Now, please let me go."

"Or what?"

Patty clenched her fist. She cocked it back. Before she could raise it, she felt another cold-warm shock. But this time, it wasn't on her arm. It was on her mouth as Deputy Sheriff Nick Newman planted his unwanted lips on hers.

CHAPTER SEVEN

"*A*re you even listening to me?"

Grizz was not listening to Mac, not even a bit. His gaze was across the room on the television screen over the bar, but his focus was decidedly fixed on Patty. Long before he'd gone into basic training, he'd mastered the art of watching out for Patricia Keaton without letting her know that he was watching her.

Back then, it had been watching her climb the monkey bars when she'd been a head smaller than the other kids. But Grizz never wanted to stunt her independence by stepping in as her safety net. So, he looked the other way.

But he always made sure there was something reflective in his eyesight so that he could see what she was up to. When they were out at the mall when she was a bit older, he'd always scan the food court and know her exact location and those surrounding her. So, watching her in the bar with that jerk of a cop while appearing to not watch her was an old hat to Grizz.

He knew she could handle herself with that buffoon of a deputy. The problem was, Grizz didn't want Newman putting his hands on her. Grizz had no idea how far Patty was willing to push him to admit his feelings for her. He was already at the end of his rope.

"Why don't you just go over there and ask her to dance," said Mac. "You're clearly not trying to get on my dance card."

"Who?" said Maggie Banks, she was the wife of Dylan Banks from the Purple Heart Ranch.

Maggie was swiping through pictures of her son to show Mac and Grizz. Grizz had smiled and nodded obediently when the mother showed him her kid. He liked kids. He often wondered what his kid would look like, especially if they had red hair, blue eyes, and an infectious giggle that made his entire body relax.

He quickly shook himself of that fantasy. He and

Patty wouldn't be together like that, much less have kids.

Would that honor go to Deputy Sheriff Newman?

Grizz watched as Patty downed her drink. The frothy concoction made him wonder if it was a virgin peanut butter cocktail, her favorite since she didn't like the sweetness of sodas. He wouldn't get an answer because she slammed the empty glass down on the table and started for the door.

"Oh, I see the boundaries of the Purple Heart Ranch are extending over to Vance Ranch again," said Maggie.

Grizz whipped his gaze back to Maggie. She and Dylan Banks had been the first couple to marry for convenience over at the rehabilitation ranch. Something or other to do with an ordinance that required only families could live full time on the land. There was no red tape on Vance Ranch.

"It's not like that," said Grizz. His fingers balled into fists as he watched Newman follow Patty out the door.

"Looks like it," said Maggie. "What's holding you up?"

"She's Keaton's baby sister," said Mac. "The whole

best friend's sister thing. I hear it's a popular story conflict in romance novels."

"It sure is." Maggie's eyes lit up. "We've had that happen at the ranch. But it was two girls who were best friends, and it was the brother that married the best friend. It's one of my favorite of our love stories. But this will be new; a boy's best friend's sister. You should definitely go for it."

"I'm not going for it," said Grizz.

"Why not?" said Maggie. "You clearly have feelings for her."

"I've known her since she was a child."

"She doesn't look like a child anymore. And she also didn't look interested in Deputy Newman. She ... wait, where did she go?"

"She left," Grizz growled.

"With Newman?"

Grizz didn't answer. He rose from his seat without another word. He was out the door in under a second.

The parking lot was dim. There weren't many people on the street at this time of night in the small town. They were either at home or in the bar unwinding. Grizz turned when he heard Patty's voice, followed by the deputy's.

Grizz walked towards the voices and then stopped in his tracks.

"You're not going anywhere until I get what I want from you."

"I gave you no signals. I'm now clearly stating that I have no interest in you. And here I'm going to use my manners and say no and thank you. Now, please let me go."

"Or what?"

Grizz got to them in time to see exactly what Deputy Newman had in mind. Patty's fist was cocked back just like he'd taught her. But Newman's hands were already on her, his lips capturing her mouth.

Patty froze.

Grizz saw red.

Patty's body stiffened. Her eyes went wide with utter shock. Her shock and dismay stunted Grizz into inaction. When Newman pulled away, there were tears in her eyes. It was Patty's tears that yanked Grizz from his stupor.

Grizz stepped to the guy. He grabbed the back of Newman's collar. Before Grizz could punch the man in his face, Newman made a choked sound like he was being strangled. Like Patty's, Grizz's cocked fist remained suspended in the air. But he knew his shock was for an entirely different reason.

Deputy Newman's lips, the lips that had stolen a kiss from Grizz's Patty, were swelling before his eyes. Newman's lips moved, but his words were gurgled, like a fish out of water. Grizz stared in fascination as Newman's lips continued to get bigger and bigger.

"A jerk," the deputy was saying. "A jerk."

"You are a jerk," said Patty, finding her voice again. She whirled the cop around, her fist still cocked. It halted when she saw his increasing lips.

"A jerk," Newman tried again, waving his hands to ward her off. He was patting his pockets, but his fingers didn't seem to be working properly. "A lure jerk."

"Yeah," said Patty. "We get it. But you're not a little jerk. You're a big jerk. That was my first kiss. It was supposed to be with Grizz. Not you. You stole it from me."

Grizz looked back at her. "Your first?"

"Yeah," she sniffed. "It was always going to be you."

"All or jerk," interrupted Newman. "Ebb E Ben."

Grizz wanted to shove the man aside. He wanted to take Patty into his arms and wipe away that tear in her eye. He wanted to hold her to him and erase the memory of anything but his own lips on hers.

Unfortunately, before that plan could be enacted, realization began to dawn.

Angel Bautista tossing peanuts on the ground at Newman's feet.

Patty's frothy drink that she'd downed before coming out here.

The continued swelling of Newman's kiss-stealing lips.

Newman was allergic to peanuts. He was having an allergic reaction. Grizz turned from Patty and began patting the deputy's pockets.

"Uh, Grizz? Why are you feeling him up when I've been coming on to you for years?"

"He's having an allergic reaction. He's allergic to peanuts."

"Serves him right for putting his mouth where it doesn't belong."

"We gotta find his EpiPen, or he could die."

Patty twisted her lips as though in thought.

"Patty."

"Fine." She sighed and went into action. "If it's not on him, maybe it's in his car. I assume that one is his."

A squad car was parked in a No Parking Zone. Grizz helped the swollen deputy to his vehicle. Once there, he let go of Newman.

The man wobbled without Grizz's shoulder to lean on. "Patty, could you?"

Patty looked at him, blue eyes aflame with irritation. She wobbled at the transfer of weight. Grizz turned quickly to get the car unlocked.

"I think he's going to pass out," said Patty.

Grizz slid the key into the lock and turned. He pulled the door open just as he heard a thud. Newman had keeled over. He'd gone down to a knee. Unfortunately, he was now in the direct line of the car door. Which Grizz had yanked open. And smacked Newman upside the head with the metal door.

Grizz and Patty looked to one another. Then down at the fallen man. Then back to each other.

"That was not on purpose," the two said in unison.

The deputy was out like a light. Unfortunately, his lips were still swelling. But he was still breathing.

"Quick, grab the EpiPen," said Grizz as he dropped to his knees to see to Newman.

Patty dashed, emerging a second later with the device. "It was in the dashboard."

Patty held the device up to the street light.

"What are you doing?" demanded Grizz.

"Trying to read the instructions," she said.

"Give it here." Grizz uncapped it and jabbed it in the man's flesh.

Newman's eyes shot open. He gasped in a deep lungful of air, glared at the two of them, and then promptly blacked out again.

This was just great. Newman would have both their hides when he came to. Grizz believed the man vindictive enough to press charges, assault with a door, or some nonsense. Worse, Patty was involved. How was he going to protect her from this?

CHAPTER EIGHT

"Newman, wake up," Grizz shouted at the prone man, still laying on the cold concrete ground.

Patty stood over the two of them, not willing to stoop down to Newman's level. None of this was her fault. He was the thief. He'd stolen her first kiss. If her mother hadn't raised her right, she'd have left him there in his own drivel.

No. She wouldn't have. She'd have punched him first and then called an ambulance. She wasn't sure if they should call one now?

The swelling on his lips had gone down. He was breathing normally instead of wheezing for breath. But his eyes remained closed.

Patty tried to muster concern for his well-being.

But she was having a difficult time at it. He still had his life, he was lucky for that. He'd stolen something precious from her.

She'd been saving herself for Grizz all her life, and Newman had come in and taken that from her. He'd put his hot-cold lips on hers. He was lucky all he got was the taste of peanuts. She'd nearly thrown up in his mouth.

"We have to call for an ambulance," said Grizz.

"Isn't the hospital just across the street?"

Grizz looked up. The lights of the emergency room flashed red in the late night. "Help me carry him."

"Me?"

"Who else? I don't want to get anyone else involved."

"Involved in what?"

"Assaulting a police officer."

"He kissed me. That wasn't my fault."

Grizz looked up at her, softening his gaze. "I know, sweetheart. I know. But, guys like him ... he could turn this around on the both of us."

"But you saw it. You saw him come on to me."

"Yes, I did."

"I didn't give him any signals other than no."

Patty took a deep breath before she started crying.

Grizz straightened, leaving Newman out cold on the ground. He wrapped his arms around Patty, enfolding her in his warmth. Patty clung to him. Inside of Grizz's embrace, her tears felt no need to fall.

"I know, Patty Cakes," Grizz sighed. "And for that, I was ready to knock him out. I'm not entirely sure I didn't purposely hit him with the car door."

"You didn't," she said into his chest, enjoying the feel of the muscles beneath his shirt.

"No, I didn't," he agreed.

Grizz was a big man, with so many muscles that he looked like his body would be hard to the touch. But inside his arms, it had always been soft as a pillow. Patty could've fallen asleep right there. Except ...

"We gotta get him some help."

Grizz pulled away from her. Patty bit her lip but didn't offer up another complaint. For now.

Between the two of them, they hefted the deputy up. Grizz did most of the heavy lifting. Patty was no shrimp. She shouldered Newman's weight on her right side. She hadn't been all too keen to help earlier. She'd had enough of Newman's hands on her before he'd fallen to the ground. But she'd keep that to herself.

"Do you really think he'll cause trouble when he wakes up?" she asked as they crossed the empty street.

"If he does, you blame the assault all on me."

"No," she said. "He'll need to take responsibility for his actions against me."

"Fine," said Grizz. "But any damage to him, we'll say that was all me."

"It was an accident."

"They might turn it into a he-said-she-said fiasco," said Grizz. "I won't let anyone put you through that."

Patty ground her molars. She wanted to drop the dead weight she was carrying right in the middle of the street. "Isn't it a he-said-she-said-he-said thing?"

Grizz scrunched up his features as he turned to her. "What?"

"It's both of our words against his."

"Him coming onto you is one thing," said Grizz as they approached the doors to the emergency room. "But the bruises on his head, the fact that he's out cold, and the delay in getting him his meds, that's where it gets hairy. He could see I approached him, ready to knock his lights out. And here he is, lights out."

"I'm not letting you take the blame for me."

Grizz ignored her as they walked into the sliding doors of the hospital. Before they could shout for help in the empty emergency room, a nurse rushed up to them.

"What happened?" asked the nurse.

"He had an allergic reaction," Grizz spoke before Patty could open her mouth. "Peanuts. We found his EpiPen and administered the dose. But he's been out for almost five minutes now."

"We'll take it from here," said the nurse, sliding Newman into a wheelchair

Patty slumped into a chair against the wall. Her shoulder ached from hefting that brute's weight. She sniffed at her shirt and cringed. His cologne was all over her. She wanted nothing more than a hot shower and to forget this night ever happened.

Grizz knelt in front of her. His gaze was soft and filled with concern as he peered into her eyes. With his thumb, he tilted up her chin.

"It's going to be okay," he said.

And just like that, everything was right once again in her world. The smell of Grizz's spicy, earthy scent filled her nostrils. That disgusting kiss had never happened. How could it when the man of her dreams brushed at her lower lip with the pad of his thumb and wiped all trace of it away.

Patty ran her fingers down his strong chin, and he let her. Grizz closed his eyes and leaned into her touch. This was what she wanted. This was what she'd always wanted. To be free to touch him, to hold him, to kiss him.

"I'll protect you," he said into her palm. "I'll always protect you."

Patty knew his words to be true. Grizz had always been her hero. She knew he would lay down his life to protect her. But she didn't want him dead or in jail. She wanted him alive, holding her hand, just like he was now.

The only thing that could make this moment more perfect would be a proposal.

"Excuse me?"

Both Patty and Grizz looked up to find the nurse who'd taken Newman back standing over them with a clipboard in hand.

"Would you and your wife mind giving us your contact information in case the doctor has some questions for you?"

"Oh," said Grizz, "We're not—"

"Of course, we don't mind." Patty took the clipboard and scribbled her phone number on the sheet. Above it, she wrote the words that had peppered so many of her high school notebooks: Mr. and Mrs. Hayes.

Patty had waited forever to have the privilege of writing that phrase. And maybe now, there was a way to make it happen.

Grizz straightened as the nurse walked back to her station. He looked from the clipboard swinging in the nurse's hand and back down to Patty.

"Did you just lie on a hospital form?" Grizz asked.

"Not necessarily," Patty said as she came to standing.

"We're not husband and wife."

"No, not right this minute. But if we were, it would solve our little problem."

"What are you talking about?

"Spousal privilege." Patty tugged him out of the sliding door. Grizz seemed so bewildered that he followed her. "There's a law where a husband and wife can't testify against each other."

"What?" Grizz pulled back from her.

"I was talking to Walter. You know, Pastor Vance. He was joking, but it's a real law. I saw it on television."

"Patty—"

"No, listen. If we get married, they can't make us testify against each other."

"I don't think that's how it works."

"You got another idea? You want to protect me? We should get married. As I hear it, people in this town get married for less."

CHAPTER NINE

*G*rizz used to hold Patty's hand all the time when she was still in pigtails. Back then, her small, chubby hand wouldn't span his large palm. He'd engulfed her, holding her delicately but securely. The security was more for him than her.

She'd gotten lost once at a county fair. Because she'd gone off and looked at the array of stuffed animals instead of following behind him. When he'd found her ten minutes later, his heart never regained its slow rhythmic beating. From that day forward, it had always sped up a bit whenever her hand wasn't in his.

Grizz's entire world slowed now that Patty's hand

was back in his grasp. She still didn't span his entire palm. But he felt her touch span his entire being.

Her palm pressed into his, and he felt swallowed. Her fingers laced with his, and he felt hooked. She gave a tug, and he went where she bade him to go. When he looked up, it was to see a large church bell.

The bell hung silently on its perch. The hour still had another quarter before the alarm needed to be sounded. Relief settled over Grizz's shoulders. There was time.

There were sins he needed to confess. The least of all were the actions back in the parking lot of the bar. The state of the deputy had been the man's own making and not a direct result of anything Grizz had done to him—not that that would be easily believed by the powers that be. But those of that particular power were men.

Grizz needed to confess his real sins to God. He needed to confess the desires he'd harbored for years for the woman whose hand he clung to. He needed to confess the actions he was seriously contemplating right now, taking her as his wife to protect her from what harm may come from earlier.

Grizz hadn't been to church in years. His temple was the cross at his neck. His congregation wherever he dropped to his knees.

When they came inside the building, it was mostly empty. He didn't see a confessional box, likely because this wasn't a Catholic church. The doors to the chapel were open. Grizz decided that would do, and headed toward the pews. But something tugged him in the other direction.

Patty.

Her blue eyes narrowed at him across their extended hands. He could've easily pulled her to him and compelled her to go where he wanted. But it was never that easy with Patty Keaton.

Patty frowned. Her bow-snapped lips pinched in a question. Grizz's answer was to come to her. Fingers still entwined, he fell in step behind her small form. A good little soldier following behind his one true cause; her protection.

There were voices down the hall, and that's the direction they walked. Patty poked her head into a room. Inside, sat a small circle of townsfolk. At the center of the circle was Walter Vance, Brenda's brother.

"When God asks Cain where his brother Abel is, we all know the response," said Pastor Vance.

"'Am I my brother's keeper,'" replied a red-headed young man.

Grizz knew the man to be Reece Cartwright.

Beside him sat a lovely woman who smiled adoringly up at him. It was Reece's wife Beth, the daughter of the town's elder pastor.

"That's exactly right, Reece," said Walter, a grin on his face.

Grizz shifted uncomfortably inside the door frame. He'd heard the story of Reece and Beth, and Walter and Beth. Beth and Walter had been engaged. But Beth had always been in love with Reece Cartwright, the soldier who'd gone missing in action a year ago and had been presumed dead. When Reece was found, they learned that his memory was lost, though not all of it. Reece had returned to his hometown, thinking that he was engaged to Beth. Beth had broken off the engagement with Walter to marry the soldier, and when Reece's memory came back, it had worked out.

There was no animosity on Walter's face as he regarded the two. Grizz didn't think he could ever handle Patty gazing adoringly at another guy.

"That answer implies that God does indeed think that Cain is responsible for his brother," Walter preached. "Now, I know this story ends in tragedy, but there's a valuable lesson hidden in here. It's not every man for himself in our society. We are tasked with the care of one another; our mothers, our fathers, our sons, our daughters, our sisters, and our brothers. We were created as a community, and we should care for all."

Around the room, the students at the nighttime Bible study nodded. Walter closed his great book with a decided thunk. "That's enough for tonight, everyone. Thank you for coming."

Reece shook Grizz's free hand as he and Beth made their way out of the door. Beth glanced back at the two of them, a knowing glint in her bright eyes. She whispered something to her husband. Reece turned to look back. The same glint lit his eyes as he chuckled and wrapped his wife in his arms.

As the others filed out of the small room, Walter made his way to Grizz and Patty. "You two missed class."

"We're not here for class," said Patty.

The young pastor looked between Patty and Grizz. Walter's gaze fastened on their joined hands. That same glint caught in the Pastor's gaze. A slow, knowing smile spread across his handsome face.

And then he groaned.

"Does it have to be today?" Walter looked down at his watch. "I had this weekend in the pool."

"What are you talking about?" asked Grizz. "What pool?"

"You know there's a pool about you two? About when you would get married."

Grizz hadn't yet allowed the thought to fully form in his own mind. But he'd allowed himself to be led here. Here, standing before a pastor to bind the one woman he shouldn't have to himself. All under the guise that it was for her protection.

"After we talked earlier," Walter was saying to Patty, "I moved my bet up to this weekend."

Grizz turned to Patty. "What did you two talk about?"

Patty didn't answer. Instead, she gripped his hand more tightly to hers.

Grizz could've easily broken free of her hold. Instead, he rubbed his thumb over her knuckles, locking her grip tighter.

"You've been here for over a week, Sergeant Hayes," said Walter. "You know how this place works with soldiers."

Grizz had heard the tales before they bought the land. But his unit didn't live on the Purple Heart Ranch, so it should not extend to him. Except here he was.

"Can't you two wait until the weekend?" asked Walter. "We could put together something special with all your family. And I could also win the bet. It's just a few days."

"I'm sorry, you're going to lose your bet," said Patty. "But do you think you can marry us tonight? Right now?"

"Why the rush?" asked the pastor. "Oh, I get it. It's your brother, isn't it? Keaton isn't on board with his best friend and his baby sister?"

Grizz gulped. He opened his mouth again. He should be the one doing the speaking. But Patty beat him to the punch again.

"That's it exactly," said Patty. "But we're in love. Have been for years."

She gazed up at Grizz. Those blue eyes that had always felt like home to him, pierced into his heart. Her words were a sieve Something punctured his chest, and all the words he never thought he could say came out of her mouth.

"I love this man with all my heart. I've always known I would spend the rest of my life with him. I've only ever wanted to be married to Grizz. To be his wife, keep his house, have his children, to be his partner."

Grizz let out a shaky breath as his heart opened wide. There was nothing left inside of him. There was nowhere left to hide his true desires.

His head felt light. Something fluttered in his belly. He was certain that the racing of his pulse would put him flat on his back.

"I love him, and I want to belong to him."

With that last proclamation, Grizz found his voice. It was the one word he tried to keep a leash on. It was the only word that was able to escape his lips now.

"Mine."

CHAPTER TEN

*I*t was happening. It was really happening. Patty was marrying the man of her dreams.

She'd felt Grizz's hands go clammy as they left the hospital. Then dry as they entered the church. They'd become warm as she professed her true, undying love for him. When she'd finally spoken her truth aloud, she'd thought he might shy away from her.

But he hadn't. He hadn't let go of her hand. He'd said that she was his.

They followed Walter down the hall to his office. The small room was more of a closet than anything else. Books wallpapered the walls. Old titles with Hebraic and Latin words on the browning spines.

It wasn't the altar she'd expected to be saying her vows at. She wasn't wearing the wedding dress of her dreams. Instead of the empire waist gown she had envisioned wearing, she was in jeans and cowboy boots. Instead of her hair being in an intricate bun woven with flowers, her tresses were in a high ponytail. Her makeup was done in dark shades designed to be seen in the low light of the bar, not the muted tones for a daytime wedding with flowers all around them.

But when it came down to it, none of that mattered. Patty was standing with Grizz about to say the words that would transform her into Mrs. Griffin Hayes. Her dream might not be in the technicolor wonder of her imagination, but it was becoming a reality. She would grab hold of it with both hands.

"Do you have the rings?" asked Pastor Vance.

Grizz and Patty looked at one another. Grizz's gaze fell to Patty's left hand and the bare fingers there. His forehead wrinkled like a problem was brewing there.

"We don't," said Grizz. "Maybe we should wait until—"

"No." Patty lifted her left hand like a five-fingered stop sign. "Remember, we already talked about how *privileged* we are to be able to do this tonight."

Patty gave Grizz a meaningful glance, a glance that she hoped would remind him of why they were rushing to get this done. She hated that her wedding dreams were finally coming true on the back of a heinous individual like Deputy Doodie Head.

She knew Grizz got her meaning when he scratched at the hairs on his chin with his right hand. Patty grabbed for his hand with her left one, entwining their fingers so that she had him on lockdown from both sides.

"Well, the ring isn't a requirement," said the pastor. "Neither is the marriage license, here in Montana. You just need to be of age, which you both are. And show that you have the mental capacity to wed."

Grizz took in another deep breath. He hadn't taken his eyes off of Patty while Pastor Vance spoke. He seemed to be searching for something. An answer? Permission?

"Patty Cakes, if we do this, it's forever. I won't ever get a divorce."

Patty's heart had been beating wildly since the moment they'd entered the church. It stopped while Grizz was talking. With her heart in arrest, it was difficult to get her lungs to work.

"Patty?"

Tears stung her eyes. Her fingers went lax, allowing Grizz to slip from her hold. But she was too weak to reclaim him.

"Sweetheart, what is it?"

Grizz's arms came around her. Patty went to him. She rested her head on his chest. The sound of his heart beating kicked hers back into gear. Her entire world homed in on the rhythm of Grizz. Her nails dug into his shirt. Her face turned into the center of his chest, and she inhaled, filling her entire being with the spicy, warm scent of him.

"You promise you won't ever leave again?" she said.

"Patty ..." Grizz sighed.

But it wasn't a sigh of exasperation. It was filled with many emotions. Some Patty didn't recognize.

Grizz brushed his fingers across her temple and then gently cupped her cheek. Patty's breath caught as he gazed down at her. There had been a time when he'd hid nothing from her. But when she'd developed boobs, he'd stopped looking at her. She'd started wearing a sports bra for a while, hoping that a uniboob would bring them back together.

It hadn't. It had taken a handful of peanuts and a stolen kiss from the wrong man to get them here. But she'd take it. When Deputy Newman woke up,

Patty would be there to thank him. That is if he wasn't trying to press charges against her.

But she didn't want to think of that jerk right now. She put her focus back on Grizz. He still held her in his arms, but she felt tension in those strong muscles of his. Instead of pulling away from her, he pulled her more tightly to his chest.

"I promise," he said.

Grizz's voice was a deep rumble. She felt the truth of his words from the crown of her head to the tips of her toes. The moment was ripe for a kiss, her true first kiss.

"So ..." Walter interrupted the tender moment. "Are we going for the standard vows?"

"No," said Patty. "I've prepared my own."

"You have?" asked Grizz.

"Of course, I have. I've been dreaming about this for years." Patty cleared her throat. She lifted her gaze and looked directly into his eyes. "Griffin Clarence Hayes."

Grizz winced. The only other person who could get away with using his middle name was Patty's mother. If Holly Keaton used a middle name when she called a kid, it could only mean one thing; run because they were in trouble.

Grizz was in trouble. He'd been caught red-handed. One of his hands was still cupping the side of Patty's face. A few strands of her red hair flowed over his fingertips.

"I've loved you since I could say your name. The first time you held my hand, I knew it was where I was supposed to spend my life. I promise to never let go of your hand. I'll be there as your strength since you've been mine. I vow to be your loving and devoted friend, partner, and wife. I look upon you without judgment, without scorn, and always with an open heart and mind."

Patty watched as Grizz's throat worked. His Adam's apple bobbed as he squinted at her. She saw his gaze glisten. Yes, this was it. Just as she'd dreamed.

"Patty, I ..." Grizz cleared his throat and tried again. "Patty, I ..." Grizz shook his head and blinked a few times. "I don't know what to say."

"I can help with that," said Pastor Vance, opening his book to the standard set of wedding vows.

"No," said Grizz. "I've got this. Patricia Anne Keaton, I knew you were special the first moment I saw you. I made it my mission to protect you. I haven't been there in a while. You've always looked at me like I was your hero, and I wasn't there for you. I'm sorry."

Patty placed her hand over the hand Grizz still had on her cheek. Then she placed her hand on his cheek. With a push of her thumb, she tilted Grizz's head back, until his gaze lifted to her again.

"If we do this," he continued, "I swear I'll be there for you every day of your life. I won't leave again. I'll protect you with my last breath."

"Those sound like perfect vows to me," said Pastor Vance. "I now pronounce you husband and wife. You may kiss your bride."

Grizz swallowed. Patty watched as his Adam's apple bobbed again and again. There was tension in his jaw, and she knew he was clenching his teeth.

Was he not going to kiss her?

She thought she'd gotten her answer when his forehead came to rest against hers. He let out a long, tortured sigh. The taste of his breath on her tongue was a cruel tease of what he would not share with her.

She'd been patient for what seemed her whole life for this man. And now he was going to hold the one last thing she wanted. He was going to make her wait and—

Grizz's lips were soft as they brushed against hers. So soft that she thought she'd imagined it. But the second touch of his lips was more than a brush, it was a press.

Slipping the hand that held her cheek down to her neck, Grizz tilted Patty's head up. He slanted his mouth over hers and deepened the kiss. It was a good thing he had a hold of her because Patty's knees went weak.

Yes, this was the kiss she'd been waiting for. Being in Grizz's arms, being claimed by his lips, was worth everything. And still, she sensed he was holding back.

She felt it in the careful way he held her. In how he broke the first and then the second touch of their lips before it could go too deep. In the way his fingers fisted at the back of her neck with a need he wasn't satiated himself with. All of that let her know there was more he had to give. He'd given her a lot with this small taste. But when she saw that there was more, she was determined to have all of that, too.

"Congratulations, Mr. and Mrs. Hayes," said Walter. "Now, good luck with telling your brother."

CHAPTER ELEVEN

*T*he ranch was quiet when they returned. The animals had settled in for the night. There were no trucks in the drive, so Grizz had to assume that the others were still out enjoying themselves at the bar.

Good. That meant he didn't have to explain where he and Patty had been. Or what they'd been up to.

Congratulations, Mr. and Mrs. Hayes.

Grizz had never thought he'd hear that title paired with his last name. His mother had gone back to her maiden name a few years after the divorce. Now, the one and only Mrs. Griffin Clarence Hayes unbuckled her seatbelt as he put the truck in park.

Patty had remained uncharacteristically quiet on

the car ride from town. She'd sat with her hands folded primly in her lap while he'd driven. She'd rested her cheek against her shoulder as she gazed out the window.

Grizz was unnerved by her calm and quiet. Patty had always been a ball of energy. Her serenity was not natural.

She waited while he came around and handed her out the car, just like he'd taught her to do. A man should always open a door for a lady. He opened the door to the house. Patty paused before stepping into the open doorway. Her gaze was trained on the ground.

Grizz looked down at the threshold of the doorway. It was a raised hump that divided the inside from the outside. When the meaning of that hump hit him, it became akin to a speed bump for his legs.

Was he supposed to carry her over the threshold? It's what a true married couple would do when entering their home for the first time as man and wife.

But this wasn't their home.

And they were man and wife only on paper. This ruse was all for her protection against that jerk of a lawman. Though ruse wasn't the right word.

Grizz had pledged to protect Patricia Keaton before she could walk. His marriage vows were simply an extension of that original oath. He would keep Patty out of harm's way, and that included if the harm came from being in his arms.

Turning his body perpendicular to the doorway, Grizz crossed his arms over his shoulders and waited for Patty to precede him into the house.

Her gaze narrowed at him in the dim light of the moon. Her lips quirked up, as though she was accepting a challenge. Angling her body towards him, she stepped across the threshold unassisted. But not before making sure to brush her body against his.

Grizz couldn't hide his sharp intake of breath. His nostrils flared as they caught the sweet scent that rested on her skin and rolled off her hair. And now Grizz knew that that same confectionary scent was what she was made of.

The honeyed taste of her from their kiss was still on his tongue. He'd been trying to forget that small sample of her. That was easily done.

It was the second helping of her that he'd stolen that knocked around in his head.

For as long as he lived, he would never forget the soft sigh that breezed over his lips. He would never forget the rightness of pulling her against him. He would never forget the peace he felt pressed against her.

He wanted to wrap himself up in her arms. He wanted to burrow his nose into her neck. He wanted another taste of her. But what shook him to his core was that, by law, he could have more. Because now, he had that privilege.

His stomach grumbled with want. He slammed the door shut to cover up the sound and headed for the kitchen.

"You hungry?" he asked.

Patty shook her head, stopping at the bottom of the staircase. "I'm ready to turn in."

It had been a long day. She was likely still reeling from her encounter with the deputy. Grizz still wished he'd had the opportunity to deck the lawless man before he'd succumbed to his allergies.

He should probably call the hospital to check in on Newman. Grizz wasn't sure how bad allergic reactions went. He was sure the man would be up soon, and then he'd likely go after Patty for revenge.

Grizz wasn't sure if this spousal privilege plan of theirs would work? But it was all they had. Now that they were married, they couldn't testify against each other. This was the only way to protect her. This was his sole job in the world, and he would not fail her.

"I'll walk you up," he said.

They barely fit together side by side as they climbed the stairs. Patty leaned into him. Then she rested her head against his shoulder, just like she'd done when she was a girl.

Her gaze was cast down. The quiet serenity remained on her face. Grizz wondered what she was thinking. He wanted a bit of that peace and quiet for himself. Instead, his mind raced.

Once they reached the second story, he stopped at her door, which was nearest to the stairs. However, Patty let go of his arm and continued on down the hall. She stopped at his bedroom door. Grizz remained at hers.

"Aren't you coming to bed?" she asked.

Grizz opened his mouth. No words would come out. His mind was a hazmat area. Yellow tape, flashing red lights, smoke clouding his vision.

He forced air into his lungs. But his words were choked when they came out. His good sense and his secret desires were locked in combat. "Patricia, that's not happening."

"Griffin, I'm your wife now." She turned the knob

on his bedroom door and stood at the edge of the threshold. "This is where I belong."

"This is not that kind of marriage. It's for your protection."

"So what? Are you planning to have it annulled after Deputy Donkey Brains wakes up, and then leave me?"

"No." Grizz was standing before her in just two long strides. "I would never leave you."

"Well, if you really want to protect me, we should make this marriage legal. The way to do that is with consummation."

Grizz shook his head. He reached for her, preparing to march her back to her room. Before he could get a hold of her, she ducked inside his room. She took a seat on his bed, toeing off her cowboy boots.

Grizz stormed into the room. He scooped her boots into his hands. Using one of her shoes, he pointed at her. "That's enough, Patty. Get off the bed. It's time for you to go to sleep."

"I'm fine sleeping right here, thank you very much."

"I'm not playing with you, Patty Cakes," Grizz growled. "I'm going to give you until the count of three and—"

"And then what?" She grinned. "You'll put me over your knee? I've read about things like that in a romance novel. Let's try it."

The boot dropped from Grizz's hand. He was sure his eyes were bugging out of his head. Exactly what had his sweet Patty Cakes been up to since he'd been away? And what had she been reading?

"What's going on here?"

Grizz cursed under his breath at the sound of his best friend's voice. If this night wasn't already trying enough. He was already at the end of his rope. And now here came a huge knot.

Grizz turned to find Keaton standing in the hall. Grizz's best friend looked between his baby sister perched, barefoot, on Grizz's bed. And then back to Grizz.

"We were wondering where you two disappeared to," said Brenda, who stood behind her husband.

"We went to church," said Patty.

"Patty, get off the man's bed," said Keaton. "You're a little too old for sleepovers."

"It's not a sleepover," said Patty scooting back on the bed. "Grizz and I are sleeping together."

Pinching the bridge of his nose, Grizz closed his eyes and let out a long, tired exhale. He hadn't figured out yet what he'd tell Keaton about all of this. He was sure once he explained the situation with Deputy Newman that there might be some understanding. With Patty's narration of the story, Grizz wasn't sure he wouldn't end up in the hospital beside the other man.

Grizz opened his eyes just in time to feel the impact of Keaton thrusting him against the wall. Keaton's calculating blue eyes were a raging storm as they bore down on Grizz.

"Keaton," shouted Patty, "let go of my husband."

"Husband?" choked Keaton.

"It's not what you think," Grizz started. And then stopped.

What was he going to tell his best friend? That he'd married his baby sister as a ruse? That it wasn't real? When Keaton had said those words to Patty, the lie had nearly burned his tongue.

Because the vows he said were real. It was his mission to protect Patty. More than anything in the world, he wanted to be her hero. And he would not leave her. Not even if she had planted herself in the middle of his bed.

"Somebody had better explain," Keaton demanded, his hold still firm on Grizz.

"You know I care about your sister," Grizz began.

"Yeah," said Keaton, tightening his hold. "Like she was your sister."

"No." Grizz shook his head. "I've had feelings for her for a while. I've been trying to keep them from you."

Grizz placed his hands over his best friends and slowly peeled them away. He met with resistance for a moment before Keaton let him go. Grizz took a deep breath and stepped a bit further on the high wire between his best friend and his wife. His feet carried him to the bed where Patty had once again taken her seat. He addressed the next bit to his wife.

"That's why I haven't dated in years. I couldn't stop thinking about Patty."

There. It was out. The words leaving his mouth were like a weight lifting off his soul.

He hadn't dated anyone since he'd almost kissed Patty three years ago. It wasn't for lack of opportunity. His mind had been so occupied with trying not to think of Patricia Keaton that he could never fit anyone else in there. Now, he wouldn't have to fight so hard anymore.

Patty's blue eyes were huge on her heart-shaped face as she regarded him. Her lips were set in a perfectly round O of wonder. She stood and took a step to him.

Grizz's heart thudded hard against his chest with each and every one of her steps. They were only about five or so steps apart. He felt lightheaded as he waited for her to get to him. Only three more steps and—

Keaton stepped between them. He turned his back on his sister and faced Grizz. "You two really got married tonight?"

"Yes." Grizz nodded.

"Legally?"

"Walter performed the ceremony at church."

Keaton took a deep breath and whistled low.

"I'm sorry we did it this way. And I'm sorry I didn't tell you what I was feeling for her. But it didn't seem appropriate because—you know—she's your sister. And I've known her all her life. And she was young. But now she's a grown woman."

Keaton balled his hand in front of Grizz's nose. It was the army signal for all motion, including talking, to halt. Ever the dutiful soldier, Grizz did as he was told.

"Wait?" said Keaton. "So, what you're telling me … is we're really brothers now?"

Grizz blinked in surprise.

Keaton clapped him on the back. Then he burst

out into laughter. "I can't believe she finally sunk her claws into you."

"Wait?" said Grizz, a bit dazed now. "You knew how I felt about her?"

"Of course, I did," said Keaton. "What? Did you think I'm clueless? I thought it would take until the summer for her to finally break you."

"I had until the end of the week," said Brenda from her post in the doorway.

CHAPTER TWELVE

*B*renda shot Patty a wink as Keaton ushered his wife out the door. The door snicked closed behind the other newlywed couple. Patty and her husband were alone again.

Grizz rubbed at his neck. The poor guy looked dazed. And bruised. The skin there was red from where Keaton had grabbed him.

Patty reached out to Grizz. He let her fingers glide over the sore spot on his neck. She felt his deep inhale. His skin was warm under her fingers. Grizz bowed his head, giving his weight over to Patty's massage.

"So, you haven't kissed another woman in three years, huh?"

Grizz's head lifted. His hazel eyes latched onto

her blue ones. His lips, which had been in a hard, pinched line, softened.

"No."

His voice was a soft growl. It made Patty's stomach rumble. She'd said she wasn't hungry before. Now her belly ached for him.

Patty ran her fingers across his shoulders. Up to his neck. Through his hair. "I can help you with that."

Patty smiled her best and brightest smile, her dimples on full display. She knew her eyes were sparkling because she felt an inner light being under Grizz's gaze.

Grizz reached up. But instead of taking her into his arms, he wove his fingers around hers and peeled them from the back of his head. "No, Patty."

Patty's stomach stopped its rumbling. Now it grumbled a hollow protest. Above her belly, her chest tightened as her heart rate slowed.

"That's not how this is going to go," he said.

"But why?" She wanted to stomp her foot. In fact, she thought she did. But her foot was bare and barely made an impact on the soft carpet. "You got Keaton's blessing. You have my permission and consent. What more do you need?"

Grizz cupped her face with his hands. Patty held

still for the embrace. How could she not? Being close to this man had been her goal for so long. The chaste kiss he pressed to her forehead, silenced her. But only for a moment.

He released her face and walked to the bed. Patty's heart kicked back into high gear. Was this it? Was it going to happen?

Grizz tore the comforter off the bed. He also snagged one of the pillows. Bending down to the floor, he began making a pallet next to the bed.

"So, we're sleeping on the floor our first night as a married couple?" asked Patty.

"I'm sleeping on the floor. You're sleeping in the bed." Grizz pulled his shirt over his head.

Patty was momentarily distracted by the revelation of his hard, corded abs and the broadness of his chest. She hadn't seen him shirtless since he'd become an Army Ranger. Whatever he'd done in his training had honed his already perfect muscles into weapons.

Grizz was still talking as he balled his shirt up and threw it into an open duffle bag on the floor. It took a second before Patty comprehended his words.

"... and you have to go back to school."

School? Was that his objection? Now would be

the perfect time to tell him that she'd dropped out of school. Problem solved.

"Yeah, Grizz, about school—"

"This marriage is not going to interfere with your education."

"Trust me," Patty slumped down on the bed, "that's not what I'm concerned about."

Patty nearly told him that she wasn't going back to school, that she hadn't been back to school in months. But she decided to focus on one argument at a time.

"Well, I am." Grizz came to the edge of the bed and knelt before her. "We were forced into this situation."

"I wasn't forced. I've wanted this my whole life."

Patty looked away from him and out the window. The moon sparkled into the dim room. She'd been told all her life not to look into the sun. She'd never understood how something so beautiful could cause so much pain. But it was fine to look into the moon because it was just a reflection of the sun. No matter how brightly the pale orb shone, it could never hurt her.

Grizz's fingers were soft as they captured her chin. Patty allowed him to turn her face to him. His dark gaze bore into hers, and she shivered.

"You know I care about you, Patty Cakes."

"You know I'm in love with you, Grizzly Bear." She shrugged. "Your move."

Grizz sighed. But the sound wasn't one of defeat. It was one of puzzlement.

"Are you trying to tell me that you don't feel anything for me?" she said.

"I do." He shut his eyes as though it was hard to look at her. "I've been telling myself for years that my feelings for you are wrong."

"They're not. They're—"

Grizz pressed a finger to her lips. It wasn't the gesture that made her hush. It was that she realized he was staring at her mouth like he might kiss her.

And then, somehow, miraculously, her prayers were answered. Grizz brushed his thumb down on the right half of her lip. With the finger gone, he made way for his lips to touch hers. It was just a light touch, the barest of caresses, but the feather-light impact was enough to knock her over. Luckily, Grizz had his arms around her.

He pulled her to him. Her head rested on his bare chest. He buried his nose into her neck and held her tight.

It was heaven. But they were still standing outside the pearly gates. Patty wanted an all-access pass. She reached between them, trying to tug at the top of her shirt.

"Hey, hey," said Grizz. "None of that."

Patty's mind raced and halted at the same moment. It was like a brain freeze, except the temperature went wonky all over her body. Unlike her horrid encounter earlier in the evening with Deputy Dunce, she was sure Grizz was giving off all the signals for Go.

So, why was he shaking his head and stilling her fumbling hands?

"I told you, we're not sleeping together," he said.

"Do you need to have a talk about what's supposed to happen between a husband and wife? I'm sure we can get Keaton back in here."

Grizz tossed his head back and laughed. When he sobered, his face was still soft with mirth. He ran his hands across her temple, pushing a lock of her hair behind her ear.

"This marriage is forever," he said. "But this relationship is new. I want to go slow."

"Slow?"

He nodded. "Maybe take you out on a date."

"You want to date?"

"Is that so strange? A husband wanting to date his wife?"

Now it was Patty's turn to pinch the bridge between her nose. Grizz took her hand in his. He turned her palm over so that her knuckles were facing him. Like a gentleman of old, he brushed a kiss across the back of her hand.

"You've been thinking about this for a long time," he said. "I haven't let myself even imagine it. Let me do it right."

In another life, this would've been cute. For someone who hadn't been waiting three years for this very moment, it might've even been romantic. For someone with patience, she might have been swept off her feet.

He wanted time? Fine, she'd give him time. But the smallest amount that she could manage it. Because Patricia Keaton—no, strike that—

Because Patricia Hayes was determined to get her man, now that she had him. She had every intention of speeding up this little courtship. But she'd play nice. For now.

"Fine," she smiled sweetly.

Grizz gave her a heart-stopping grin of his own, and Patty nearly tossed her resolve. But when he pulled away from her and slipped under the comforter on the floor, her determination shifted into high gear.

Patty slipped one of the straps of her shirt off her shoulders. Grizz's smile slipped as he watched her. His eyes went wider than saucers. He sat bolt up, giving Patty another delicious view of his strong chest and defined six-pack.

"What are you doing?" he demanded.

"Getting ready for bed like you said."

"You can't take off your clothes." He held up his hands, as though they were a stop sign.

Patty ignored his directions. "You did."

Grizz pursed his lips again. She'd missed this, the teasing between them. Even though it had never been on this level with articles of clothing coming off. Now, she'd get to tease him and see his bare chest for the rest of her life. It was a win-win any way she looked at it.

Patty slid the other strap down her shoulder. Grizz followed the fall of the fabric. He shut his eyes tight. Then he turned his back for good measure.

Patty stood and shimmied out of her jeans and shirt. She walked across the room, skirting the pallet he'd made on the floor.

"Patricia," he growled as she came near him.

"Relax," she said. "I'm just getting something to sleep in."

She picked up his discarded shirt from his duffle

bag and slipped it over her head. Grizz's scent surrounded her. The shirt was still warm from his body heat. It was the next best thing to being in his arms, which clearly wasn't happening tonight.

Which was fine. There was tomorrow. Then the night after that until forever.

"Okay," she said, once she was under the covers in his bed. "I'm decent."

Grizz opened first one and then the other eye. His throat worked as he took in what he saw.

"Is this going to be our life together?" she mused. "Separate bedrooms like in those old shows you used to watch?"

"Those were the good old times," he said. "Wanna watch one?"

"Sure," she sighed. "Since I doubt there's anything higher than PG-rated that you want to do."

CHAPTER THIRTEEN

Grizz's dreams were fevered that night. The taste of Patty lingered on his tongue. His palms itched to be full of her. Her sweet scent filled his head every time he inhaled. Her soft sighs of rest crashed into his ears all his waking hours.

She was so close, yet so far.

He spent most of the night gazing up at her from his place on the floor. Her arm lay curled on the pillow. Her cheek rested heavily in the crook of her elbow. The cloud of red hair rested on her shoulders. Her beautiful features were soft under cover of night.

Grizz wanted to run his fingers over the fine hairs

at her temple. He wanted to brush his lips across her closed eyelids. He wanted ... her.

The scary thing was that he could have her.

She was his wife. His partner. His responsibility. From now until forever.

For years, he'd fought against this particular desire in his heart. Now, it was served up to him on a firm mattress. He need only rise and take what had been freely offered up to him.

Grizz rolled over and came to his haunches. He paused in a low crouch as Patty shifted in bed. Holding his breath and keeping perfectly still during surveillance as his army training had taught him, Grizz waited for Patty to settle. When she did, he rose to his full height, towering over her.

The war was over. The tugging at his heart had been decided. This slip of a woman had unmanned him, and he was admittedly, daresay happily, at her mercy. He just wasn't ready for the victory celebration, as it were.

If he was going to do this, he was going to do it right. Patty deserved a courtship, complete with roses and flowers and romantic poems. She also deserved a man who could take care of her financially. So, with that final thought in mind, Grizz grabbed a clean set of clothes and slipped out of their bedroom.

The cold shower did nothing for him. Not even when he opened his eyes to let the water in. The deluge did not wipe away the vision of Patty, the taste of her, the feel of her.

Grizz wanted his wife.

Instead, he went out to the field and threw his body into manual labor. He'd never fancied himself a rancher, but he liked the physicality of the daily chores. Like Keaton, Brenda had a running list of chores, but only one ranch hand; Angel. Grizz, Keaton, and Mac tried to fill in whenever possible, but with the training camp opening date looming, they couldn't help out as much as they'd like. And with the theft the other day, things had been in an uproar.

Grizz grabbed a box of tools and headed to one of the pastures. Manuel Bautista had managed to free Brenda's young calves from this enclosure and steal them off the ranch while they'd all slept. The enclosure had been a fence Grizz had fixed on his second day here.

Brenda had insisted that none of this was Grizz's fault. Conceptually, Grizz understood that. It hadn't been his shoddy mending work. It had been all Bautista.

Still, in his heart, Grizz felt responsible for nearly losing Brenda her livelihood. Taking out his tools, Grizz worked the hammer and nails to ensure that the young calves would not be separated from them again.

He hadn't learned any of his mending and repair skills from his father. What Grizz knew of construction, he'd learn by watching other men, paying attention to lessons in school, or his training in the army.

What he knew of maintaining a healthy relationship and making a marriage work, he solely knew from the old black and white television shows he'd watched growing up. No, Mr. Cleaver hadn't mended fences or baled hay. But the man had held down a steady job and taken care of his family.

How was Grizz going to do that when he was broke? Sure, his mother was out from under the debt his father had saddled her with after the divorce. That effort had taken Grizz's last cent. Grizz had no problem living hand to mouth. But he couldn't expect his wife and family to do so.

Grizz cursed as the nail slipped, and he hit his

thumb. His wife and family. He hadn't even thought about having children. How was he going to take care of his wife and kids?

"What are you doing up so early?"

Grizz turned to see Keaton headed his way. Instead of his normal cargo pants and combat boots, the soldier was decked out in worn jeans and cowboy boots. His typically close-cropped hair was curling around his ears. The man was glowing with the aftermath that could only come from being a newlywed.

"I figured you'd still be in bed with ..." Keaton stopped there. His throat worked like a cat with a hairball about to come stateside. The skin at Keaton's neck turned green.

Here was the awkwardness Grizz had been expecting would spring up between himself and his best friend ever since Grizz had noticed that Patty Cakes wasn't a little girl anymore.

"We didn't—" Grizz started.

"Stop." Keaton waved his hands like a frantic red pentagon sign.

"But me and Patty-"

"No, no means no."

Keaton boxed his ears with his hands. He closed

his eyes and shook his head like he did when they were boys, and Ron and Hermione shared their first kiss. Keaton didn't want to play wizards and quidditch after that literary moment. He'd also begun to get suspicious of books after slogging through that deathly hollow. Young Grizz had been secretly rooting for the two friends to finally admit to their feelings, and he'd silently cheered when it was displayed between the book's covers.

Right now, Grizz could do nothing but stand and wait for his friend to grow up. Besides, Keaton was right. He didn't need to know the ins and outs of Grizz and Patty's marriage, nor where in the bedroom Grizz had slept last night. His and Patty's was a real marriage, and it would be consummated in due time. After Grizz got his proverbial house in order.

Keaton peeled open one eye. Whatever he saw in Grizz's annoyed countenance must have made him believe all was clear because Keaton opened the other eye and removed his hands from his ears.

"You done?" asked Grizz.

Keaton gave himself one final shake. "Even though I knew this day would come, I don't want to hear any of the details."

"Deal," said Grizz. "You headed over to the camp?"

"Not yet. Maggie's coming by to check on the bull."

"The prize bull who ran into your Jeep?"

"That would be the one."

When Keaton had first visited the ranch, Brenda's brand new breeding bull had gotten out of his pen—courtesy of one Manuel Bautista—and rammed right into Keaton's rental car. Both man and bull had gone down. Keaton was back on his feet, but the bull was laid down in one of the pastures. Its ears were lowered, and its tail was tucked between its legs. Even Grizz, who had no degree in animal husbandry, knew those weren't good signs.

"Brenda doesn't think he'll be able to do his job," Keaton continued.

Keaton grimaced at the assignment. So did Grizz. A bull's job was to breed every female put in its pasture. Both Grizz and Keaton had always been one-woman kind of men. All of the men in their unit were. They were each loyal to a fault.

Grizz turned in the direction of another field where cows and calves were rising in search of the day's sustenance. The females ushered their calves to the choicest spots in the pasture, but it wouldn't be enough. The land was already patchy and barren in spots.

Angel Bautista made his way over to the pasture. On his back, he'd hefted a bag of feed. The feed was to supplement the livestock's diet. The color of the bag reminded Grizz of the sacks of food his mother would get from the neighborhood donation's food pantry when times had gotten rough, and his father was nowhere to be found.

"I've been meaning to ask you," said Keaton, "how's it going recouping that last payment from the defense contract work?"

All of the men in their unit had been severed from the Army at the same time. Each had taken a bit of a break before coming and starting work on the camp. But Grizz had decided to spend a couple of weeks on a contract assignment to make a few extra bucks to pay his share of the investment into the camp. He was still waiting for those funds to come in.

He'd used his last penny to pay off the final debts that his father had left on his mother. Writing that check had made his chest puff up. Now, his chest deflated as his hands patted his empty pockets.

"Still hasn't come through yet?" Keaton clapped him on the back. "I know how these things work.

Don't worry. We can just take it out of the profits from the first clients."

It was a kind gesture. The kind of gesture made between brothers. Grizz had no doubt that any of the others in their unit would've made the same offer. Heck, he would've extended the same hand had one of his fellow soldiers been dealt a similar blow.

But it wasn't just about Grizz anymore. Now he had a wife. And he had to care for her. He would not be going to any donations pantry or handout cupboard to take care of Patty. Before Grizz could refuse, Mac popped his curly head from behind the barn.

"I figured you'd still be in bed with your new wife," said Mac.

"Aww, man." Keaton grabbed his stomach and headed away from the two men.

Mac laughed as he watched Patty's brother run off. "Thanks for that, I'm a few bucks richer. I won the bet. I knew the moment little old Patty Cakes turned up here, you were a goner."

Grizz opened his mouth to tell Mac it was none of his business when his cellphone went off. He walked a few paces and answered it. In just an instant, Grizz's ire at his friend was gone. His chagrin over the charity Keaton had offered was put on the back burner.

"Sergeant Hayes? This is Sheriff Declan. We need you to come down and answer some questions about Deputy Newman."

CHAPTER FOURTEEN

Smoke wafted up to the ceiling in the kitchen. The white walls turned a light shade of gray that darkened as the contents in the pan continued to burn. Patty went to the window. Finding the latch, she shoved it open.

The dark curls of smoke made a mad dash to escape. But the late afternoon breeze pushed them back into the kitchen. The acrid smell pushed inside Patty's nose, and she let out a string of coughs. She pressed a dish towel to her face. Then waved it about in an effort to urge the smoke to clear. Eventually, it did dissipate, but the smell lingered.

The veggies in the pan were no longer green. They were black. The long strips she'd cut were all stiff at the edges but soggy in the middle. They were limp with rigor mortis as she moved the pan from the stove to the sink and turned on the tap.

"Darn, you too?"

Patty looked up. Her new sister-in-law stood in the back door, holding it open to usher out more of the singed stench. Brenda was dressed in a pair of jeans that molded to her form. Also molded on her form was mud at her ankles and grass stains on her knees. But Brenda still looked beautiful with her windswept hair and sun-kissed skin.

Brenda was a pretty tomboy, the kind of girl Patty had loved playing with on the playground when she was younger. But Patty had traded her sneakers for kitten heels and her cut-off jeans for sundresses. All in an effort to be Grizz's perfect sitcom wife.

Here she was, Mrs. Griffin Hayes. She was dressed in a sundress that flared from her hips but also had butter stains on the bodice. Her demure bun was unraveling on her shoulders. She'd kicked off her heels just before her failed rescue attempt of the vegetables.

"I'm sorry about this," said Patty. "I'll get it cleaned up.

"I was hoping you'd be the wife who could cook," Brenda said as she came into the kitchen. "I can slaughter the beef. I just can't cook it."

"Oh, no." Patty gave a shake of her head, her curls bouncing happily around her shoulders as though thrilled to be set free. She bent over to the oven where a timer was set to go off in another ten seconds. Patty opened the door and pulled out a perfectly cooked roast. "Meat I can handle. It's just the veggies that always bite the dust under my spatula."

Brenda's nostrils flared in what looked like delight. "I'm a meat and potatoes girl, too. Green is for the cows."

"My thoughts exactly." Patty put the perfectly cooked roast on the stove. The herbs and spices of the meat quickly overpowered the burned veggie stench. "The cows eat the grass, so aren't we getting the benefit of that."

"No," grinned Brenda. "But I love the way you think."

Brenda's eyes lit up like she was looking at her own reflection in a mirror that flattered her appearance. Patty saw her old self when she looked at Brenda. She missed the girl who ran and laughed for days without a care for what boys thought.

"So," said Brenda, reaching for the coffee maker. "You got hitched last night."

Patty pulled the apron over her head. After she

balled the buttered up garment into a ball, she nodded in response to Brenda's rhetorical statement. Instead of words, Patty waited to see where her new sister would take this.

"Why?" said Brenda. "I mean, I know you're in love with Grizz."

"You do?"

"It's clear as day. It's clear he has feelings for you, too."

"It is?"

Brenda pulled out a coffee mug and filled it to the brim with steaming dark roast. "What I don't understand is why now?"

Patty tugged at her lower lip. She wanted someone to talk with this about. All her girlfriends from high school had gone off to different places, and they hadn't kept in touch. She didn't have any girlfriends at college since she hadn't been there for months, and hadn't been invested in it since she'd stepped foot on campus. She looked up to her new sister-in-law, wondering if she could trust Brenda with her many secrets.

"I know this place gets to you," said Brenda after a long sip. She turned to the open window and looked out at the lush scenery. "People always said there's something in the land. I never believed it until I met your brother and married him all in the same day."

"Yeah." Patty turned her gaze out to the greenery of the ranch. "Keaton always said he had a five-year plan. And then he got hitched in a day."

"So, what's your and Grizz's story? What happened to get you two down the aisle so fast and with no family present?"

Brenda turned her gaze back to Patty. Her green eyes were friendly. But then they dipped to Patty's flat belly.

"No." Patty covered her stomach. "Nothing like that."

Patty chewed at her lip another second before spilling the beans. The beans of that night of her high school graduation where Grizz had almost kissed her. The beans of last night with Deputy Dog Food. The beans where she and Grizz wound up at the church standing before Brenda's brother. But not the beans about college and her lack of attendance there.

"So, let me get this straight," said Brenda. "You two got married because you assaulted a police officer?"

"We didn't assault him. Newman assaulted me. But it would be his word against mine. Grizz wanted to make sure they couldn't make us testify against each other, and a husband and wife can't testify against one another, so ..."

"Yeah," said Brenda after another healthy sip of her coffee, "I don't think it works like that."

"Too late. We're married. But now I need him to act like we're married. He won't come near me."

"Keaton and I—"

"Ew." Patty threw her hands over her ears. "I do not want to hear about you and my brother. Ew ew ew."

"I was only going to say that Keaton and I had planned a platonic relationship. But after a few days, that went out the window."

"Nope. Still not hearing you."

"All I'm saying is that, like our marriage, your marriage to Grizz happened quick. You gotta give it time. You two also haven't seen each other for years. You need to spend some time getting to know who you are now. I'm sure you both have changed in the time you've been apart."

They had. There were things Patty didn't know about Grizz. And there were definitely things Grizz didn't know about her.

Patty wished they still had the ease with which they'd had when they were younger.

"This roast is going to make a great dinner," said Brenda. "But the guys won't be back for another hour or so. Wanna help me with the calves?"

"Sure."

"You'll need to change out of that homemaker getup." Brenda frowned at the sundress Patty wore. "You got a pair of jeans you don't mind ruining?"

CHAPTER FIFTEEN

Grizz parked the truck. Despite living on the poor side of town and growing up without his own father, Grizz had never been on the wrong side of the law. He'd never seen the inside of a jail cell, nor a police precinct.

Taking a deep breath, Grizz hefted himself out of the truck. He hadn't given Mac or Keaton any of the details of why the sheriff was calling, nor of what had happened before his impromptu wedding last night. He figured he'd handle one thing at a time. Grizz was just thankful that the sheriff had only called him down and not Patty. If there was going to be any trouble, he wanted to be in front of it and have her far out of harm's way.

That was why he'd married her, after all. To keep her out of trouble.

Honestly, that line wasn't flying anymore. Grizz had married Patty because he'd wanted her. He'd wanted her the second she'd become a legal adult. And now that he had her, he wasn't going to give her up easily.

Newman had assaulted his wife. The handsy jerk had kissed Patty without her permission or her invitation. What had happened after that—the delay in delivering the EpiPen dose, the knock on the head with the car door—had been a series of unfortunate events. But events preempted by Newman.

That's what he'd tell the sheriff today. It was Newman's actions. Not Grizz's wife's.

"Excuse me, sir?"

Grizz looked down, and then down some more. Standing before him was an older woman. A cloud of gray hair surrounded her round face. Her eyes were dim, with dark circles under them. It looked as though she'd been crying. Grizz's instincts to protect any woman who looked as though she'd worked her fingers to the bone kicked in.

"Yes, ma'am? What do you need? What can I do for you?"

She offered him a wane smile. "You're the soldier from Bellflower Ranch?"

The Bellflower Ranch was the original name of The Purple Heart Ranch, so called because a bellflower resembled the teardrop emblem of the decorative military award.

"I'm one of the soldiers that work there, yes, ma'am."

"Are you the one who helped my boy the other night?"

"Your boy?"

The older woman nodded. "My poor Nick."

Nick? Nick Newman? As in Deputy Nick Newman, who stole Patty's first kiss away from Grizz.

"I just want to thank you so much for looking after my son the other night."

Mrs. Newman patted Grizz on the back of his hand. Grizz fought the urge to pull away from her. She held firm. Her gaze filled with gratitude and appreciation. And now, Grizz fought the grimace that wanted to crawl over his features.

"Ever since his father left, little Nicky's had a hard time," Mrs. Newman continued. "Especially in the social arena."

Somehow, that fact did not surprise Grizz. Grizz had seen up close that the guy didn't get along with people he perceived were different from him, like Angel Bautista. Grizz also remembered the cop's tacky pickup lines that he'd aimed at Patty. Newman hadn't even been able to read the fact that Patty wasn't interested in him.

"I'm so glad he's found a friend like you."

Grizz gave an internal shake. Then his hands shook, finally wrenching himself free of Mrs. Newman's grasp. When his head began to shake, he stopped. There was a tear in Mrs. Newman's eye.

She dabbed at it with an index finger. Her gaze downcast as she spoke. "Now, we just have to pray that he wakes up."

Pray that he wakes up?

"He's still unconscious?" asked Grizz.

Mrs. Newman nodded. "I do hope you'll stop by the hospital later. I'm sure it'll help to hear a friendly voice to coax him out of the coma."

Coma?

Mrs. Newman patted Grizz's hand. Then she cupped his face and smiled. "I'll bet your mama's proud of you."

Grizz stood in the hall for long minutes after she'd left. He was stunned at the turn of events. Newman was still out cold. And somehow, Grizz had been cast not as a villain but as the hero and protector of the real bad guy.

He wanted to rail against this role. But he couldn't open his mouth. Something held him back.

Grizz watched as Mrs. Newman climbed into a beat-up Honda Civic. She slid the key into the ignition, took a deep breath, and let it out. As she let out the breath, she also allowed her features to crumble.

There had only been a few times when Grizz had caught his mother crying. Each time had broken something inside him and reinforced his determination to pick up the slack that had been dropped by his father. His mother's tears were also the reason why Grizz had never found himself in any trouble with authorities.

"Sergeant Hayes?"

Grizz turned to see Sheriff Declan making his way to him. The sheriff didn't smile. But neither did he look over Grizz with suspicion. The dark-skinned man offered Grizz his hand, and Grizz shook it.

"I'm sorry to bring you out here," Declan began. "We just had a few gaps we wanted to fill in. Since you and Ms. Keaton were the only ones—"

"Mrs. Hayes," Grizz corrected. "Patricia Keaton is my wife."

"Oh." Declan's brows rose. "I didn't know the two of you were married."

"We were married the other night. We were on our way to Pastor Vance when we came across Deputy Newman having some trouble in the parking lot."

"I had heard from the bartender that the three of you left together," said Declan.

"Patty and I left together." It wasn't exactly a lie. Grizz had followed Patty out when he'd seen Newman trailing her. "Deputy Newman was in the parking lot at the same time as we were."

"The bartender also said that Ms. Keaton— forgive me, Mrs. Hayes spent a lot of time talking with Deputy Newman."

Declan's un-accusing, unsmiling features remained placid. Grizz made sure his face gave off the same message.

"Patty's a friendly girl," said Grizz. "She's always made friends wherever she goes."

"So, there was no ... tension between you and Deputy Newman?"

"Absolutely not," said Grizz. "I know how my wife feels about me. And she knows how I feel about her. There is no tension in our marriage. If there may have been unrequited feelings on the part of

Deputy Newman, you'll have to ask him when he wakes up. But, when we saw the man in need, my wife and I did everything in our power to help him."

Grizz nearly bit his tongue on that last stretch. Both he and Patty had hesitated to offer their immediate assistance. But only for a moment. And then they'd launched into action.

True, their actions had led to the bump on the man's head, but it was the best they could do under the circumstances.

"Do you have any other details you care to give, Sergeant Hayes?"

Grizz shook his head at the sheriff. "That's all I saw. Deputy Newman was having an allergic reaction. I found his EpiPen and administered the dose."

"I was going to call Mrs. Hayes down for questioning." The sheriff scribbled on the pad, but it didn't look as though the letters made any sense. "But as you're her husband, I assume you'll have the same story."

It was a rhetorical question, and so Grizz didn't answer it. He would do anything to ensure that Patty was safe and out of harm's way. If that meant that he would get in trouble for her with the law, then so be it. That's what a husband should do for his wife.

That's what any man should do for a woman he cared about.

It grated that with the details Grizz had left out, it would mean that Newman would get away unscathed for what he'd done to Patty. But Grizz was taking no chances.

Newman may have stolen a kiss from her untouched lips, but he'd nearly paid with his life. As far as Grizz was concerned, Newman had gotten off easy with the allergic reaction, the bump, and the day, or more, in bed. When the deputy woke up, if he wanted to make trouble, Grizz would be there to shield Patty.

"If that's all," said Grizz, "I'd like to get back to my wife. We're still newlyweds."

The sheriff looked up with a genuine smile this time. "Congratulations. I'll be in touch when Deputy Newman wakes up. In case there's anything else we need from you or Mrs. Hayes."

Grizz nodded and made his way out of the doors. He knew he hadn't heard the end of this. But he had a brief reprieve from the intrusion of Nick Newman in his life. And he knew exactly what he was going to do with his time.

The drive back to the ranch seemed longer. Grizz knew why. He was eager to get back to his wife.

There was nothing standing in his way from dating Patty. So, that was his plan. He'd go in and ask his wife on a date.

His palms sweat as he came up the steps to the back door of the big house. Patty had grown into such a polished young woman. She was always entirely put together from what she wore, to how she spoke, to her hair. She truly resembled the women in the sitcoms he'd loved as a child. They'd always seemed unattainable to Grizz, like a fantasy.

Coming up to the door, Grizz smelled the makings of a delicious feast. Pastor Vance must have come over again to cook. Grizz knew that Brenda had no cooking skills. And if he remembered correctly, Patty wasn't a whizz in the kitchen either. Unless it was to cook hamburgers or steak.

Through the screen of the door, Grizz saw a woman bent over the oven. She wore a pair of cutoff jeans. Her feet were bare. Her hair was down around her shoulders.

She looked nothing like the unattainable fantasy of June Cleaver. She looked like the girl next door. The girl a guy could pal around with one minute, and tell his deepest secrets to the next minute.

The woman straightened, and Grizz saw Patty.

But she wasn't the Patty he'd married. She was the Patty he'd known as a girl.

Patty startled when she saw him, nearly dropping the pan in her hands.

Grizz rushed into action, taking the dish from her and setting it on the stovetop.

"Hey," she said.

"Hey," he mimed.

"I didn't expect you back so early."

Grizz could only stare. This wasn't his fantasy. This was the real Patty. The girl he'd sat and watched those black and white shows with. The girl he could talk to about anything.

Most importantly, this was the woman he dared not dream of. And here she was, standing within his reach.

"I look a mess," she said. "I've been out with Brenda all afternoon on the ranch. And now, I've just finished with dinner. Let me go change into something presentable."

"No." Grizz put his hand out, catching her at her midriff. "You look beautiful."

"I look a mess."

"You look like you."

Patty's lips parted. For the first time, Grizz didn't

feel the need to run from what he was feeling, to run from her. So, he pulled her to him.

She inhaled sharply as she came to his chest, her heart pressing into his. Her eyes widened, taking all of him in. Her head tilted back, offering herself to him.

Grizz brushed his lips against Patty's. He urged himself to be patient. To take his time with her. To take his time with himself.

But he didn't.

He'd waited so long for this. Denied himself for too much time. Now, he would take what had always been his.

Patty didn't resist. She wrapped her arms around his neck and pulled him down to her. Grizz went willingly. He'd always been wrapped around her finger. Now, he was wrapped around her entire being.

"Patricia?" he said when he finally broke away from her.

"Yes, Griffin?"

"Would you like to go on a date with me?"

She grinned, her eyes shining bright in the setting sunlight. "Sure. I'm available for the rest of my life."

CHAPTER SIXTEEN

*P*atty's heart raced. Her palms were hot. Her breath came fast. She was on a date with Grizz. Sure, they were just sitting on the back porch of the Vance ranch house. But she'd take what she could get.

Much like her wedding, the date wasn't what she had envisioned. First, because he wouldn't let her change her outfit. Grizz insisted that he liked the way she looked. There was grease splattered on her shirt, and her hair was in a messy ponytail. Still, he looked at her as though she were the most beautiful thing in the world. Patty decided to wash and wear the same thing again tomorrow, and then again the next day. Anything to keep him looking at her like that.

She wasn't in one of the flaring sundresses she'd seen Mrs. Cleaver wear. Nor kitten heels that she'd seen Donna Reed putter around the kitchen in. Patty was dressed in a T-shirt and cutoff jeans from helping Brenda earlier in the day with the calves.

Patty had been a natural at herding the small beasts into a new pasture. The separation from their mothers signaled that the calves were grown and had to now make it on their own. Patty, sure enough, understood that. She'd been on her own for the last few months, having unenrolled herself from college and taken the odd job here and there. The monies from the last year of her college tuition sat in a bank untouched until she could gather up the courage to tell her mother what she'd done.

Not that she needed to tell her mother anything. Her father had left Patty that money. True, it had been earmarked for her education. But it hadn't mattered to anyone that going to college wasn't high on Patty's list. It wasn't even on her list.

Patty had only ever had one thing on her future to-do list. And she was doing exactly that. She was finally doing what she knew she was born to do, serving her husband a well-cooked meal after a hard day of work.

"You never did meet a vegetable you liked," said Grizz.

He grinned as he watched her push around the salad on her plate. The only reason the leaves were granted an appearance on the porcelain was because that's what the sitcom housewives would've done. Patty had dumped a cup of dressing over the greens. However, she still pushed the limp leaves around her plate.

Grizz reached over and speared her vegetables with his fork. He lifted the dripping bit of salad into his mouth, plopped it on his tongue, and chewed.

Patty watched the action, reaffirming her dislike of veggies. How had those green devils of the earth managed to slip into the spot she coveted most?

"Where is everyone?" he asked.

"Brenda and Keaton went for a ride. Mac is over at the Purple Heart Ranch hanging with the guys there."

"So, it's just you and me?"

Patty nodded, liking the sound of that. Then she bit at the bottom of her lip. "Is that okay?"

"Of course, it's okay," Grizz said, cocking his head to the side to look at her.

"It's just ..." Patty tugged at the top of her lip. "I

wasn't sure you wanted to hang out with me. You keep leaving."

Grizz let out a long sigh. He set his utensils down and reached for her hands. Patty, who'd already eaten all of the meat from her plate, happily put aside the remaining vegetables to take Grizz's hands.

"I'm sorry, Patty Cakes. I know we haven't started this marriage off on the right foot. But all that's going to change now."

"It is?"

Grizz nodded. His hazel eyes bored into hers. Patty had to hold herself still.

It had been so long since he'd let her see past his walls. But now he sat before her, his walls were down. His arms open. He still held her away, but maybe he'd finally bring her inside his embrace.

Grizz opened his mouth to speak. But then he closed it. His gaze narrowed as he focused on something just to the right of her left eye. "You have a mole there."

Patty touched the corner of her left eye, feeling the raised skin there. "Yeah."

"That hasn't always been there."

"No," she said. "It showed up when I was around seventeen or so."

"Figures." Grizz's gaze flicked back to her. "That

was around the time I stopped looking directly at you."

He was right. They'd been so close all through her childhood. He'd been her hero, her protector, her friend. And then it all stopped, and he left.

Softness touched the side of her face. Grizz's thumb rubbed at the mole. His large hand cupped her cheek.

"I'm sorry I did that," he said. "That I tried to stay away from you."

"It hurt," she admitted.

"It hurt me, too. Especially when you were always the one person I wanted to spend my days with. It was always going to be you for me."

"I told you so." Her eyes flashed up at him.

The golden flecks in his gaze twinkled with delight. "Sure, when you were seven, and I was ten."

"I was very wise for my age."

Patty rubbed her cheek in Grizz's palm. The span of his hand was so big that she had more than enough space to do it. She could've made a pillow of his hand if he let her, and he was letting her.

Grizz's fingers curled around the back of her head. With a gentle yet insistent tug, he pulled her to him. The twinkle in his eyes caught fire.

"I'm never going to leave you again," he said. "I

love you, Patricia Anne Keaton Hayes."

Patty closed her eyes. She wanted to—no, needed to look away from him. The intensity of the emotions on her face was going to knock her down.

Was this why he'd looked away from her as she'd gotten older? Was this why he'd stayed away? She understood the depth of what he was feeling at this moment because she'd been rolling around in it for years. Having it aimed at her now was too much.

"Will you marry me?"

Patty's eyes slammed open. "I already married you."

Grizz shook his head slowly. His eyes were fastened to her lips. Patty knew she was going to be kissed by her husband, kissed very soon and very well.

"No," he said. "I mean a proper wedding. Outside with the sun shining. You in a white gown that's high-waisted and flowing. Your hair all done up with flowers woven in. And family and friends all around us."

He'd just described the wedding of her dreams. A tear trickled down Patty's cheek. Grizz caught the droplet with his thumb and wiped it away.

"Yes," she breathed. "Yes," she said louder. "Ye—"

She was about to shout it so that everyone in the

next twenty miles heard her, but Grizz captured her lips. Her shout was pressed between them. She gave him her answer for the third time as he tilted her head back and claimed her mouth. She accepted his proposal again and again as he deepened the kiss. Her arms wrapped around him in a vow of forever. She would have and hold this man from this day forward, and she dared sickness, poverty, or even death to try and come between them.

Grizz was all smiles when he finally broke the kiss after long moments. Patty had not gotten her fill. The sun was still setting, and she wanted to explore more of her wifely duties upstairs. But Grizz seemed in no rush to claim her in all the ways that he could.

"We'll plan for a May wedding," he was saying.

"Why so far away?"

"I don't want it to interrupt your studies," he said. "Your graduation is on the seventeenth of May, right?"

The school's graduation day was set for that particular day. However, Patty would not be walking across that stage.

"Yeah," Patty cringed. "About that ..."

"About what?" Grizz rubbed his thumb back and forth across her chin, his smile was indulgent as he focused more on her lips than the words.

"School," said Patty.

"What about school?"

"Well, there's good news and bad news."

Grizz's thumb stopped its motion, and his gaze rose to meet hers. "Give me the bad news first."

"The good news," she said, ignoring him, "is that we don't have to waste money on weekend conjugal visits."

Grizz narrowed his gaze. "Why not?"

"Well, that's the bad news."

"Patricia ..."

"I dropped out of college."

Grizz sighed, shaking his head. "You are not dropping out of college. We can make this marriage work. We probably need the distance to get to know each other as we are now and—"

"You're not hearing me," Patty interrupted. "I spoke in the past tense."

Grizz cocked his head. He turned his body so that he was facing her head-on. "You dropped out?"

Patty nodded.

"Right before you came here?"

"Well ..."

"When, Patty?"

"The end of last term."

"December?" Grizz sprung to his feet, his boots

making a thudding sound as he marched the length of the porch and back to her. "Your mother is going to kill you. You know that, right? And then she's going to kill me."

"On the bright side, we'll die together."

Grizz scowled at her.

"You said 'til death do us part," Patty chided.

"With your mother, it'll definitely be death."

"So what?" Patty shrugged. "You won't be her favorite anymore. Maybe she can dote on her blood-born children for a while."

Grizz scrubbed a hand over his beard, clearly not listening to her. He paced the porch length a second time. He stopped in front of Patty with his index finger raised as though he had an idea.

"We need to call her," he said.

"Oh, no." Now it was Patty's turn to rise and begin her own march. "I'm not dying a virgin."

She made a dash for the stairs that led to the pastures. Grizz caught her around the waist before she could get far. His hold was like iron. In any other instance, Patty would've loved being in his embrace. This was the only time where she fought it.

"Okay, fine," she said. "But, you're telling her."

"Why me?"

"You're my husband. You need to protect me."

CHAPTER SEVENTEEN

Grizz's ear still rang from the tongue-lashing Mrs. Keaton had given them. Patty had gotten the worst of it. Grizz suspected the only reason he got off a smidge easy was that he truly was Mrs. Keaton's favorite amongst the three of them. And now, he truly was her child.

He could hear the happiness in Holly Keaton's voice beneath the scolding. She appeared more upset that she hadn't been a part of either of her children's weddings. But Grizz promised to make up for it by letting her, Patty, and Brenda plan a double wedding this summer, as big and as grand as she pleased. Grizz couldn't say no to the woman who had helped raise him and showed him what real family looked like.

What he did worry about was how to pay for the wedding, plus pay his fair share for the camp, and now taking care of a wife.

He rose the next morning, back stiff from his place on the floor. Despite much coaxing and pouting from his wife, Grizz had insisted on keeping their wedding night sleeping arrangements. He had thought of putting Patty back in her old room, but they'd both vetoed the idea, needing to be close to one another. In the same room if not in the same bed.

Before she'd climbed onto the bed, Grizz had brushed a stray strand of hair out of Patty's face. His face had dipped low to hers. He'd brushed his lips over hers.

Grizz didn't press the kiss. No, that was her. She pressed her lips into him, desperate to take in more of him. Grizz had growled against his wife's lips and pulled back.

"Slow down," he'd said. "We're taking this step by step."

"What if I want to leap?"

"You should know, Mrs. Hayes, that I'm not that kind of man."

Patty had pouted. Once upon a time, Grizz had

bowed to her plump lips. Now, he stole a kiss from them.

"This is important to me," he said. "You're important to me. I want to get this right."

"We're right together. I don't think we can go wrong."

He'd twined their fingers together. "Here's my plan. We take it slow over the next week. We go on a few dates. Ending with nothing more than a few kisses."

Patty rolled her eyes, ready to protest. "I'm sure I'm the only wife in the world who has to seduce her husband."

"Not seduce," said Grizz, rolling his body out on the nest on the floor. "I want to be wooed. Flowers, candy, the works. Are you hearing me, Mrs. Hayes?"

He'd gotten a pillow thrown to the chest for that. He'd laughed and caught it. They had gazed at each other, talking quietly until Patty had fallen asleep. It had been just like old times.

The sun peeked above the horizon when he sat up. It had been a restful night of sleep. Likely because he felt at home for the first time in a long time. He had his best friend's blessing, his maternal figure's enthusiasm, and there was his wife lying comfortably in the bed beside him.

Grizz took a moment to simply gaze at his wife. He'd watched Patty sleep many times before. Whether it was waking her up from a deep slumber when they were young or having her fall asleep beside him when they watched a movie in the family room. Patty wasn't a night person as much as she wasn't an early riser. She liked her sleep and would keep her eyes closed for as long as she possibly could.

Grizz took advantage of that fact now as he gazed at her. Her features were soft in her repose. Her hands were wrapped around her pillow as though it was a lover she refused to let go of. She had kicked off the sheets in the night, and her long legs were on display for him. Her lashes kissed the tops of her cheeks, and Grizz became jealous.

He leaned over and brushed a soft kiss to her cheek. She smelled of sweetness with a hint of spice. Her eyes fluttered open, and Grizz felt caught in their depths.

A slow smile spread across her face. She tilted her head up. She didn't crash her lips into his like she had the other day. She waited, as though seeing if he'd meet her halfway.

Like a moth to a flame, he came to her. He brushed his lips lightly over hers. Warmth spread through him. All the stiffness from lying on the floor left him on an exhale. He leaned into her, pressing his chest against hers.

Deepening the kiss, he took his first real taste of her on this, the first day of the rest of their wedded bliss. Joy spread through him as he realized he could do this every day, at any moment, for as long as he liked. He'd lived in a black and white world for so long, but Patty brought color to his life.

She wrapped her arms around him. She tugged him to her, on top of her. Grizz wanted to go. He wanted to devour her. But he pulled himself away. He needed to remember the plan.

What was the plan?

Right. Go slow. Court her. Earn her love.

"I love you, Grizz."

Well, didn't that seal the deal? He had her love.

"This is my dream come true," she said against his lips.

Grizz realized it was his dream too. He'd never dared to see her face in his mind. Still, he'd known that for the last few years, it had always been her. It may have always been her.

Grizz bent his head and tasted her again. She was his dream. His reality. His wife. With that knowledge, the plan went out the window.

With the plan interrupted a knock came at the door. Grizz cursed under his breath as he pulled away from the small piece of heaven that was his Patricia Hayes.

"Go away," she called, bringing a grin to Grizz's lips.

"Whatever you're doing, I don't want to know," said Keaton. "But someone's here at the door for you."

"Then tell them to go away," said Patty as she reached for Grizz.

"It's the sheriff."

Both Patty and Grizz pulled away then. Grizz watched Patty's throat work as the same gulp went down his throat.

CHAPTER EIGHTEEN

*G*rizz held her hand as they walked down the stairs. His fingers were crushing hers, but Patty didn't complain. Whatever was about to happen, they would face this together as husband and wife, a united front that the law couldn't pull apart.

Grizz let go of her hand and offered his to the sheriff standing in the large living room.

"Good to see you again, Sergeant Hayes," said the sheriff.

"You too, Sheriff Declan."

Again? When had Grizz seen him the first time? Keaton and Brenda sat side by side on a small couch. Mac leaned against the fireplace.

"Any change in Deputy Newman?" asked Grizz. "Has he come out of the coma?"

Coma? When had Newman slipped into a coma? And how come Grizz knew and didn't tell her?

"He's awake, but still a bit out of it." The sheriff's eyes came to settle on Patty. "Your name came up, Mrs. Hayes."

"Me?" asked Patty.

The sheriff's gaze went back to Grizz. "I just have a few questions to ask your wife if she wouldn't mind coming down to the precinct."

Grizz took a step back and put his hand at Patty's low back. Keaton stood at Grizz's right shoulder. Brenda's hand was in Keaton's. Mac pushed off the fireplace, taking lazy steps toward them.

"Can't you question her here, Sheriff Declan?" asked Brenda.

"I want to make it plain," said the sheriff, holding up his hands. "Mrs. Hayes isn't under arrest. There are just a few discrepancies in the story your husband told and what Deputy Newman is saying. We want to get them straight."

"I'm not testifying against my husband," said Patty. "We have spousal privilege."

The sheriff quirked an eyebrow. As did Keaton. But unlike the sheriff, Keaton had more practice in schooling his features when he thought his little sister was up to something, and he wanted in on the plan.

"As I said," said the sheriff, "no one is under arrest. And I don't believe spousal privilege works that way."

"It doesn't matter if privilege applies or not," said Grizz, squeezing Patty's hand. "If you want to talk to my wife, it'll be with me present."

The sheriff looked Grizz up and down. Patty knew that if this became a physical thing that the two men were equally matched. The sheriff had the same big barrel chest as Grizz. The two men shared the same determined grimace. But the sheriff would best Grizz was with the gun at his hip and the badge at his chest.

"Grizz, it's fine," said Patty. "I'll go. Neither of us did anything wrong. We tried to help despite ... everything."

Patty saw the flicker of interest in the sheriff's eyes at her words. Oh, man. She was not going to do well in this little chat.

"You want to tell me what really happened that night?" said the sheriff.

Patty inhaled. "I didn't do anything wrong. Neither did my husband."

"But your husband left something out of the story, didn't he? There was a bump on Deputy Newman's head. Know anything about that?"

"That was my fault," said Patty and Grizz at the same time.

The sheriff looked between the two.

"We tried to help him to his car," said Grizz. "To get the EpiPen."

"He was on me," said Patty. "But he's a big guy, and I couldn't hold his weight."

"On you?" asked the sheriff.

"Leaning on her," said Grizz. "I went to search for the EpiPen in the dashboard. Patty couldn't carry his weight, and he fell. That's when I pulled the door open, and it smacked him in the head."

"It was not on purpose," said Patty. "It's not like my husband assaulted *him*."

Again, the sheriff's gaze flickered with interest at her words. Well, the single word at the end of her statement and the inflection she'd put on it.

"And that's it?" asked the sheriff. "That's all you have to add, Mrs. Hayes?"

Patty felt like Sheriff Declan was her history professor trying to coax more about the Battle of 1812 out of her. She didn't care about long ago fights. She could never remember the details.

Except she could remember the feel of Newman's cold hands on her. The smell of his beer-laced breath. The unwanted touch of his lips as they crashed against her mouth.

Patty was sorry that Newman had suffered a medical consequence because of it. She'd much preferred to knock his lights out with her fists instead of her lips. But here they were.

Her gaze caught Grizz's. Patty knew that he could tell what she was thinking. His jaw clenched. She knew that if she didn't keep her mouth shut, he would tell all. And then try and take any of the blame that came.

"No," said Patty. "That's all that happened."

"Deputy Newman is saying that you assaulted him," said the sheriff.

"Grizz didn't do anything," Patty insisted. "He's the one that got the EpiPen and dragged Newman to the emergency room."

"No," said the sheriff. "Not your husband. You, Mrs. Hayes. Deputy Newman said that you assaulted him."

CHAPTER NINETEEN

Grizz's truck came to a screeching halt. If he'd thought he'd gotten an earful from Mrs. Keaton, he was getting a heaping second helping from her daughter. Patty could hardly contain herself on the drive over to the hospital.

"*I* assaulted *him*?"

Patty stomped her foot against the floorboards of the truck. Hard enough that for a moment, Grizz thought the vehicle might break. He sped up after the light went green and took a left turn.

"He kissed *me*." Patty jabbed a thumb at her chest.

"I know, sweetheart." Grizz slowed even more as

he took a right turn into town. He liked the feel of that pet name in his mouth.

Patty turned to him as he paused at a stoplight. "You saw us in the bar, right? I was not giving off any signals."

"I know, beautiful."

Grizz let that word roll around his tongue as he turned into the hospital parking lot. He decided he liked sweetheart more. It wasn't Patty's looks that had won him over. It was her spirit, her wit, her strength, and tenacity.

"I'm going to kill him," she growled.

Before Grizz could put the vehicle in park, Patty was already tugging at the door handle. She marched toward the sliding glass doors like a soldier stomping into battle. Grizz hopped out of the driver's side and dashed to her side.

"Honeybun," he tried.

But she eluded his grasp, likely because the pet name wasn't familiar to her yet. Grizz got his arms around her waist just as she reached the reception area. That didn't slow her down.

"Deputy Newman's room?" Patty demanded of the haggard nurse at the desk.

Was it Grizz's imagination? Or did the nurse

shudder before she told them a number and pointed to a door at the end of the hall? With even more determination, Patty marched to the room. And paused.

"Slide it on in there, honeybuns."

Inside the room, Nick Newman sat propped up on pillows. A tray of nondescript hospital food was over his lap. Another nurse was spoon-feeding him jiggly, red Jell-O. The look on the nurse's face told Grizz that she was nearing ready to write herself a pink slip. Grizz determined never to call Patty honeybun again.

Newman, whose mouth had been opened wide to receive the congealed square, shut when he spied his visitors. A predatory smile spread over his face when he saw Patty. But when Newman glanced over his shoulders, his gaze narrowed.

"What's he doing here?" asked Nick.

"He's my husband."

"Your husband." Newman sat up higher in the bed, nearly spilling the blobs of Jell-O on the sheets.

The nurse took the opportunity to slip out of the room. Grizz moved aside, giving the nurse a sympathetic grimace. He'd only encountered Newman twice. That first time when he'd tried to lump Angel Bautista in the same category as his villainous uncle, which Grizz was certain was due to racial prejudice. And then again, when the deputy had tried to put the moves on Patty. Each time, the man had tried Grizz's patience.

"You never said you were married," said Newman.

"I also never said I was interested in you."

Newman's gaze slid to Grizz. "Looks like your wife was trying to make an adulterer out of me along with her assault?"

"Assault?" Now it was Grizz who stepped into the room, shielding Patty from any more of this nonsense. He'd been prepared to be the voice of reason, but he was fast losing his patience with this man for the third time. "You put your unwanted lips on my wife's mouth."

"And you knew I had an allergy," said Newman. "Looks premeditated to me."

"You just don't know when to stop," said Grizz. "Do you?"

"I wasn't the married woman flirting with another guy," said Newman. "Hey wait, you said she was your sister."

"I said she was my best friend's sister," said Grizz.

"And I wasn't flirting with you," said Patty. She tried to shove around Grizz's shoulders to get at Newman, but having his wife actually assault this dirtbag was the last thing either of them needed.

"All you women are the same," Newman sneered. "You'll lead a man on and then jerk away when we reach out."

Grizz was nearly across the threshold, ready to throttle the man in his sickbed. A quavering voice behind him stopped him in his tracks.

"Nicky, how dare you say such things."

"Mama?" All the color drained from Newman's face, and he looked truly ill.

Grizz turned to see the gray bun of Mrs. Newman behind Patty. Beside Mrs. Newman stood Sheriff Declan.

Mrs. Newman stepped forward, her small stature loomed large the room. "These people helped you. I thought they were your friends."

"She's the reason I'm here." Newman pointed at Patty. "She at peanuts before I kissed her."

"You kissed her?" Sheriff Declan stood just beyond the door. But his booming voice resonated over all of their heads.

"She led me on," Newman insisted.

"I did no such thing," said Patty.

Grizz looked at the sheriff's calculating eyes. Grizz noted that there wasn't much surprise there. Had the sheriff known that this was his deputy's behavior? Had this been the something more he'd been trying to prod out of Grizz and Patty during his questioning?

Inside Grizz's embrace, Patty was stewing. Her bright blue eyes the hottest part of a deadly fire. It was clear the person she wanted to burn with the flame was lying in the hospital bed. Grizz had half a mind to let her go and claw Newman's eyes out.

Then Grizz's gaze landed on Mrs. Newman. The lines around her eyes looked tired, weary. Her fingers trembled as she clutched at her worn purse. Her back was straight, but her shoulders hunched. In that pose, she reminded Grizz very much of his mother.

Grizz hadn't given his mother much trouble after his father left. He'd watched her work her fingers to the bones going from one back-breaking job in the morning to another at night. When she did pause a moment to look at her son, Grizz saw the worry in her gaze that she wasn't enough to bring the boy into manhood.

"I did not raise you like this," Mrs. Newman said. "You apologize immediately."

"But—"

Newman's protest was cut off with one sharp glance from his mother. Her shoulders snapped back. Her hands balled into fists. Grizz knew this look, too. He'd seen it most often on the face of Mrs. Keaton. It meant *I brought you into this world, and I can take you out.*

Newman's gaze swung to Patty and Grizz. "It's come to my attention that I may have offended you."

"You think," said Patty.

"Patricia," Grizz chastised his wife.

"Thank you, Deputy Newman," Patty said through gritted teeth.

Sheriff Declan stepped past the two of them and entered the room. "Newman, you'll be taking a leave of absence from the force."

"What?" said Newman. "Why?"

"This isn't the first time there's been a complaint," said Declan. "And not just by a woman. By citizens of different racial and religious backgrounds than you as well. You're going to undergo sensitivity training with HR."

"So, I take it, there will be no more questions for me or my wife?" said Grizz.

"No," said Declan. "You and Mrs. Hayes are free to go."

Back in the truck, Grizz pulled Patty's seatbelt tight across her torso. The sound of the metal clicking into place and locking her in was very satisfying. With her strapped to the seat, he pressed a kiss to her lips.

Patty tried to lean toward him, but the belt wouldn't let her get any closer. She let out a frustrated groan, which made him chuckle.

She was well and truly his. There was nothing standing in their way. No threats looming over them. Well, besides the one where he wasn't sure how he would provide for her.

Grizz had no plans to live off her brother's charity. He'd take a job in town to pay his fair share and to take care of her. He would figure something out. In the meantime, he reveled in the sweet taste of her lips.

"Could this count as a date?" she asked.

"Coming to the hospital?"

"We drove from home. There was some discussion. And now we're kissing. All we need is some food and flowers, and I think it qualifies."

"No, this is not how I plan to wine and dine my wife."

"Your wife does not need to be wined and dined. You're the one that wants to be wooed."

Grizz chuckled at that. He leaned in for another kiss. As his lips touched hers, he had serious thoughts of revising his plan to do this all properly. Nothing had been traditional about this marriage so far. Why start now?

CHAPTER TWENTY

*P*atty was delighted as Grizz kissed her for long moments in the parking lot of the hospital. He kissed her even longer when they'd parked on the ranch. He was still kissing her when there was a knock at the truck's window.

Mac grinned into the driver's side window. Grizz growled, murderously low. The low and beastly rumble didn't wipe the cheek from Mac's grin.

"I know the honeymoon isn't over yet," said Mac. "But your presence is needed at the camp. We're already behind Keaton's crazy schedule, and we need to go over an order for new supplies that weren't in the original budget."

"How much?" Grizzled growled even lower.

Mac shrugged. "Shouldn't be more than a grand after we split it six ways."

"I'll be over in a bit." Grizz sighed as if the weight of the world just came down on his shoulders. After Mac left, Grizz leaned his head back against the headrest in what looked like defeat.

Patty ran her fingers through his hair. It was getting longer now that he wasn't regularly cutting it for the army.

"What's wrong?" she asked.

"Nothing for you to worry about," he said, taking her hand and kissing it.

"Is it the setback at the camp?"

"No, we'll get through that."

"Then what? The money?"

He didn't answer.

"If you need money, you can just use mine."

He lowered his head and looked at her as though she'd just eaten a frog right in front of him. Patty couldn't fathom why? They were married now. What was hers was his.

"I haven't touched most of the money set aside for my senior year of college," she went on. "There's more than enough. You can use it to buy what you need."

"I'm not taking your money."

"It's not my money, it's our money."

"That's the money your parents set aside for your college education."

"Which I never wanted. It was wasted." And then she laughed. "Even without the degree, I still got my dream job. Hey, I am going to want a ring, you know."

"Patricia, no. That is not happening."

"You're not getting me a ring?"

"No." He pulled all the way back from her, slumping in the driver's seat. "Not the ring. I'm not taking your money."

"Why not? Think of it like a dowry of old times. Didn't men marry women based on the size of the money that came with her?"

Grizz's expression soured as though that idea were the foulest lemon he'd ever come in contact with. "I'll take on more defense contract work before I let you lift a finger to support this family."

Now it was Patty's turn to lean back against the passenger side window. "While I appreciate the offer of being a pampered wife, I have no intention of having my husband leave me again for who knows how long and go into some danger zone when I have the money we need sitting untouched in a bank account."

"It would be short term," he said. "Nothing more than a couple of months at most."

"You already promised you'd stay." Patty's bottom lip was already trembling. She'd just gotten him, and now she was going to lose him again. Over something preventable. He was making this choice to leave.

Grizz reached for her hands, but she pulled them away from him. Instead, she reached for the car door handle. As she opened the door, she wondered, was this another metaphor? They said as one door opens, another closes.

She heard the car door slam from the other side of the vehicle. But she was already racing for yet another door. Patty reached the front door of the ranch house and wrenched it open.

She didn't look back to see if Grizz was following her or not. She was truly unsure if he would follow. She raced up the stairs and into their shared bedroom, slamming the door behind her, but leaving it unlocked.

Sometime later, there was a quiet knock at the closed bedroom door. She knew it wasn't Grizz. He might knock, but his large hands didn't know how to be that quiet. Patty had expected Brenda to come to her. She went to the door and found that she was wrong.

Keaton stood on the other side of the door. His hand was raised, fist balled, preparing to knock again. "Can I come in?"

Patty looked past her brother. She didn't see his wife. Nor did Patty see her husband. Leaving the door wide open, Patty went back inside and slumped down on the bed.

She wasn't in the mood for one of her brother's chastising talks. She was in the mood to yell at someone. She'd give Keaton a minute to tell her she was wrong for running away from yet another problem, and then she'd lay in on him.

Keaton sat beside her. His arm lifted and went around her. At first, Patty stiffened. Where was the chastisement? Where were his words about her being irresponsible and not thinking? Instead, he brushed a quick kiss to the side of her forehead.

"Not as easy as you thought it would be, huh?" he said. "He's not an easy man to live with. I should know. I camped out in the desert with him."

Tears threatened Patty's eyes. Keaton's features changed, darkening from jovial to murder.

"Wait." Keaton pulled away from her. "What did

he do? Did he hurt you? Did he do ... something you didn't like?"

"What? No. We haven't even slept in the same bed yet. He's been sleeping on the floor."

Keaton turned to look at the floor as though he didn't understand her meaning.

"I know what you're going to say." Patty buried her head in her brother's chest. "That I'm running away from my problems."

"I wasn't going to say that."

"That I shouldn't have dropped out of school."

"You dropped out of school? Does Mom know?"

"That I shouldn't have run from what happened with Deputy Newman and tricked Grizz into marrying me."

"You what? Why am I just hearing this?"

"And that I shouldn't have run from him now. That I should've stayed and talked it out. But he's going to leave me."

"Trust me, if I know anything, it's that Grizz is not going to leave you. He's crazy about you. Has been since we were all kids."

"But he's going to leave to do another contract job because he has no money, and he won't take mine."

"Well, that's just stupid."

"Wait?" Patty looked up at her brother. "You're agreeing with me?"

"Your plan is more sound than his. So, yeah, I'm agreeing with you."

"But he's going to leave me again."

"Again? When did he leave you the first time? Do you mean when we joined the Army Rangers?"

"He didn't come back when you did for breaks."

"Patty, that was because he had feelings for you, and he didn't think he should. He was right. He shouldn't have. He's never looked at a woman the way he looks at you. He never dated in school or when we were in the armed forces. I think it was always you for him."

"He never dated anyone?"

Keaton shook his head. "He always said it was because he had no interest in marrying. And, honestly, I believed that about him. That's really why I thought he stayed away from you because he thought he'd fail like his father did. That's his biggest fear, becoming his father and leaving a woman to shoulder the financial burden of a family. So, yeah, it makes sense that he won't let you pay his way."

"But that's not how family works."

"I know. You know." Keaton left the third

sentence, the one that would invoke Grizz knowing, unsaid. Because he didn't know.

"How do I fix this?" Patty asked her big brother.

"I don't think you can. It's a guy thing. Let me talk to him."

CHAPTER TWENTY-ONE

Grizz didn't follow Patty into the house. What more could he say? He'd spent so much of his life protecting her, making sure she had everything she needed. But she was right. He had kept his distance. It was the way he knew to care for her.

It was just that he no longer wanted to keep his distance from her. Being apart from his wife, the woman he loved—had loved all his life—made him physically ill. But what could be done? He needed to provide for her, and this was the only way he knew how.

As a kid, Grizz had watched his mother work her fingers to the bone. She had taken to ignoring him. He'd received the love and attention he needed from the Keaton family. Mr. Keaton had shown him what it looked like to take care of a family by going away and deploying to dangerous places. Mrs. Keaton had shown him what it was like to have a mother fuss over him. A young Keaton had shown him what it was like to have a brother who would die for him. And Patty?

Patty had shown him the purest form of love. Patricia Keaton had shown Grizz what it was like to be loved unconditionally, just for who he was. For that, he wanted to give her the world, even if it meant that his life might be forfeited because of it.

Why couldn't she see that that was how he loved her? That was how he'd always loved her. How he always would love her.

"You're breaking her heart, you know."

Grizz couldn't raise his head to meet his best friend's gaze. This was what he'd tried to avoid all these years. This particular confrontation.

"You're breaking mine, too," Keaton continued.

That brought Grizz's head up. "What did I do to you?"

"We said we were out. And now I see you're going back in. Why?"

"Because I'm broke," Grizz finally admitted. "I can't pay my share for the camp. I can't take care of my wife. I have to go back in. It's what a man would do."

"You're an idiot, you know that?"

Grizz wanted to growl. He wanted to punch Keaton in the nose. His best friend had always had things easy; a mother at home, a father who was there, and enough food in the pantry to never worry about going hungry. At Grizz's house, they didn't have a pantry. Everything fit in the fridge or the few cupboards beside it.

"You should've come to the rest of us," Keaton continued. "You should've told us. At the very least, you should've told me. You know I would've covered you."

Grizz was already shaking his head before Keaton finished his sentence. But Keaton would have none of it.

"Don't give me this charity thing again," Keaton scoffed. "You're my brother. Legally now. You've always been family, and this is what family does for each other. This is what Rangers do for one another. We never let one of our brothers fall."

"That's life or death in combat zones."

"And marriage is different how?"

Grizz struggled for a response. He and Patty had already navigated so many minefields this past week.

Bombs had gone off at every turn in their relationship. At the end of the day, Grizz did not want to lose this war.

"We've had women taking care of us since before we were born," said Keaton. "Besides, isn't that what they did in those old books of yours; families paid to have their daughters taken off their hands. It's a small price to pay for me to have you deal with Patty for the rest of your life."

But it still wasn't sitting well with Grizz.

"Fine." Keaton pulled out his cell phone. "Then you call my mother and tell her that my sister dropped out, was nearly arrested for assaulting an officer, and is about to be abandoned by her husband after a couple days of marriage."

Grizz cringed away from the phone.

"Actually, no, I'll call her." Keaton brought the phone back to himself. "It's about time I get back on the pedestal as her favorite son. This will definitely knock you off."

Grizz smacked the phone from his best friend's hand. Keaton lifted his brow in mockery. Then Keaton reached for Grizz and brought him into an embrace.

"We're in this together, buddy," said Keaton.

When they pulled away, Keaton punched him in the gut. Grizz doubled over.

"That's for making my sister cry."

"Duly noted," Grizz choked.

By the time he climbed the stairs to their room, Grizz had recovered his breath. Grizz reached for the door just as it opened. Patty stood on the other side. Her eyes were red, her cheeks puffy, her upper lip stiff as she regarded him.

"Hey," he said.

"Hey," she said.

They stood gazing at each other from across the barrier of the threshold.

"Griffin, I want to tell you exactly what's on my mind."

"Okay, Patty Cakes."

"I don't need your protection. I'm a capable woman."

"I know you're more than capable."

"If you don't want to take my money, fine. But you're not in this alone. I'm going to work alongside you."

"No." Grizz gave a determined shake of his head. Patty sighed.

"I have a better idea," he continued. "We're going to use your money and buy our own house."

Patty blinked. Then she gave a shake of her head as though to make sure she'd heard him correctly. "We are?"

"We can buy something in town, or build it here on the ranch together."

His wife's eyes lit up like the sky after a storm. Glimmers of sunlight sparkled through like rays of hope. Grizz's heart burst open at the sight of it.

"So, you're not going away?" she said.

"No," he said. "I promised. I'm never leaving you again. I love you too much for that."

Patty closed her eyes as though saying a prayer. "I love you too, Grizz."

"I'm sorry," he said. "I'm just so used to taking care of you, that I didn't take a moment to ask if this is what you wanted. But it's going to mean a lot of late nights working on the camp, and maybe even an odd job or two in town. But it will be temporary. Meanwhile, you'll get to live out your dream as a housewife."

"My dream was always to marry you. I achieved that."

She was his dream, one he hadn't dared to think would ever come true. But there she stood. All he needed do was cross the threshold and take what was his.

Patty beat him to it. She leaped over the threshold of the door and right into his arms. Grizz caught her, as he always would. He didn't take a step back. He absorbed her weight. And then he took a definitive step across the bedroom's barrier.

Their lips came together in a heated, possessive kiss. Grizz took possession of what was his, while his wife took possession of what had always been hers. They wrapped themselves around one another, any plans of a long courtship now going out the window.

With a kick of his boot, Grizz pressed the door closed. With the bedroom door closed, all the possibilities for their future lay open before them. Another quiet snick of the lock, and he and his wife made their way into the bedroom. Both eager to make this marriage permanent in every way that mattered.

EPILOGUE

A soft series of dings preceded Mac Kenzie as he shouldered into the door of the establishment. He looked up to find two small white bells tied together with a white ribbon hanging over the entryway. Wedding bells. Fitting as he'd entered a wedding dress shop.

Mac walked into the storeroom as though walking through a cloudy sky of satin, tulle, and a polyester blend of white. Most men would've shrunk back in fear at the sight. Most men would've never crossed the threshold, to begin with. Mac wasn't most men.

It wasn't like he frequented wedding shops. Though when he was in a grocery or convenience store, he might've lingered looking at *Today's*

Bride and *Destination Wedding* magazines. It was a habit. His mother was a wedding planner, so he'd been around it his whole life.

He loved watching two people design the start of their lives together. The colors they chose to represent their love. Where they planned to put themselves on display. The menu and cakes they choose to feed their loved ones. You could tell so much about a couple in whether chose a live band or a DJ to host their reception.

The shop proprietress looked up from her phone call and gave him a cheery smile. Mac sat a smoothie container on the counter. She smiled at him gratefully and waved him towards the back.

Mac clutched the other three drinks close to his chest, careful not to spill a drop on any of the gowns on the rack, as he made his way to the backroom; the inner sanctum where brides made the most important choice of their married lives.

Most men did not tread here. Most fiancés didn't anyway. This was a place for sisters, girlfriends, and mothers.

The two women in wedding gowns were both already married. Brenda Keaton and Patty Hayes twirled around in white gowns. Both of their mothers were on their way. Mac, carrying the knowledge of his mother, was a stand-in.

That, and he was their ride. Both of their husbands had foisted the chore on Mac in exchange for doing all of Mac's chores on the army training camp they were building together. Mac was certain he got the better end of the deal.

Brenda and Patty beamed at their reflections in the mirror. Mac winked at Patty in her empire waist gown. It was perfect for her curvy body. But the cut-out patterned dress that Brenda wore didn't sit well on her tall, athletic frame.

"What?" asked Brenda. "You don't like it?"

"No, I do," said Mac. "It's just with your figure and your height, you should go for a princess cut dress."

Mac turned to the stash of dresses he'd laid out before going and grabbing the girls' drinks. He pulled aside the last dress he'd picked out. His fingers had lingered over the dress because it was so familiar to him. Another tall, athletic girl had chosen a similar dress to wear years ago. The fact that Mac had seen it was likely the reason she'd run before their wedding day.

Mac shook off the memory. Not enough to put Lana out of his mind. She was a permanent fixture there. And he had every hope that one day soon, she'd come out of his mind and be with him in reality.

She'd run from him then, and he'd let her. His father had taught him that a caged bird might accept its captor, but what it would always want was flight. Best to open the door and hope that it would return home each day.

And so Mac had opened the door and allowed the love of his life her freedom. He was still waiting for her to return home to him. Truth be told, he was close to hunting her down and dragging her back to him.

But not today. Today, he would help his friends' wives plan the wedding of their dreams. Then maybe, someday soon, he'd have the wedding of his dreams.

Mac turned to Brenda, dress in hand.

Brenda's eyes lit up. "Our new friend just tried on that same dress."

"Your new friend?" asked Mac.

"Yes, I think she said she was a reporter," said Brenda. "Oh, there she is now."

The dressing room door off to the far right opened and a woman stepped out. She had light, bird-like steps that indicated that she might fly away at any moment. Her body was tall and lean. The princess cut dress highlighted the length of her long limbs, making her look both regal and again.

Mac's heart fluttered in his chest as recognition dawned. He was yanked back in time, two years ago. The night he'd seen the woman he loved in her wedding gown. The worst night of his life. The night she chose her career over him. The night she flew out of his life.

"Lana?" he said.

Lana's head jerked up. Her gaze connected with Mac as recognition began to dawn. She gave herself a shake, like a bird whose feathers were ruffled. Her head made tiny, incremental movements as though she couldn't believe what she was seeing.

She inhaled deeply, holding her limbs taut as though readying herself to take flight. And then she bolted out the back door.

Make no mistake that this will be the last time that Lana runs from Mac.
Wanna see how this Army Ranger catches the woman he loves?
Grab your copy of
The Rancher takes his Runaway Bride.

Shanae Johnson was raised by Saturday Morning cartoons and After School Specials. She still doesn't understand why there isn't a life lesson that ties the issues of the day together just before bedtime. While she's still waiting for the meaning of it all, she writes stories to try and figure it all out. Her books are wholesome and sweet, but her are heroes are hot and heroines are full of sass!

And by the way, the E elongates the A. So it's pronounced Shan-aaaaaaaa. Perfect for a hero to call out across the moors, or up to a balcony, or to blare outside her window on a boombox. If you hear him calling her name, please send him her way!

You can sign up for Shanae's Reader Group at
http://bit.ly/ShanaeJohnsonReaders

Also By Shanae Johnson

The Rangers of Purple Heart
The Rancher takes his Convenient Bride
The Rancher takes his Best Friend's Sister

The Rancher takes his Runaway Bride

The Rancher takes his Star Crossed Love

The Rancher takes his Love at First Sight

The Rancher takes his Last Chance at Love

The Brides of Purple Heart

On His Bended Knee

Hand Over His Heart

Offering His Arm

His Permanent Scar

Having His Back

In Over His Head

Always On His Mind

Every Step He Takes

In His Good Hands

Light Up His Life

Strength to Stand

The Rebel Royals series

The King and the Kindergarten Teacher

The Prince and the Pie Maker

The Duke and the DJ

The Marquis and the Magician's Assistant

The Princess and the Principal